Inside Voices

Inside Voices
The Fiction Desk Anthology Series
Volume Sixteen

Edited by Rob Redman

The Fiction Desk

First published in 2024 by The Fiction Desk Ltd.

This collection © The Fiction Desk Ltd.
Individual stories © their respective authors.

This book is sold subject to the condition that it shall not, by the way of trade or otherwise, be lent, resold, hired out, or otherwise circulated without the publisher's prior consent in any form of binding or cover other than that in which it is published and without a similar condition, including this condition, being imposed on the subsequent purchaser.

ISBN 978-1-0686641-0-6

The stories contained within this volume are works of fiction. Any resemblence between people or businesses depicted in these stories and those existing in the real world is entirely coincidental.

Please see our website for current contact
details and submissions information.

www.thefictiondesk.com

Printed and bound in the UK by Imprint Digital.

Contents

Introduction *Rob Redman*	7
Inside Voices *Jo Gatford*	9
Mayflies *Alastair Chisholm*	21
Book Burning *David Malvina*	33
The Business at Tradeston *Eva Carson*	41
Black Hill *Lauren O'Donoghue*	71
Ghost Walks *Ian Critchley*	83
The Loop *Tina Morganella*	91
About the Contributors	97

Introduction
Rob Redman

Just as we were getting this anthology ready for press, a survey commissioned by the Reading Agency revealed that more than a third of adults in the UK have given up reading for pleasure.

Participants in the survey gave various reasons for this: life events, health issues, difficulty finding anything they actually want to read, and of course the distraction of social media. Alarmingly, one recurring theme is people having difficulty concentrating on reading for more than a few minutes at a time.

Tempting as it is to get lost in a round of hand-wringing – because, after all, what *is* the world coming to? – might I instead propose a solution? It's a pretty obvious one. I expect it's occurred to you already, given what you're doing right now.

Short stories.

Although they're very much a niche interest these days, short stories really are the perfect form to address the challenges of reading in modern life: at its best, a story can create a world, fill it with ideas and vividly real people, and take you on a journey, in less time than it takes to bake a lasagne. An anthology like the one you're holding in your hands can introduce a whole range of styles, ideas, and stories in a package small enough to, well, to hold in your hands. It's the perfect way to rediscover — or indeed discover for the first time — a love of reading.

Between them, the stories in these pages contain so much of what is good about reading: ideas, adventures, empathy. Just look at the depth of the two main characters and their relationship that Jo Gatford conjures up in twelve pages in our title story, or the unforgettably vivid characterisation that Lauren O'Donoghue gives us in her story, or the unreal real world created by Alastair Chisholm — or if you want something just a little longer, take a trip with Eva Carson through the unsettling supernatural mysteries of a Glasgow industrial estate.

It has always been an honour and a privilege to work with authors of the calibre that we feature in our anthologies, but working with authors is only part of a publisher's role: we also have to make the case for reading. And not just our own books, but reading as an activity, a hobby, a way of life. Judging by the Reading Agency's survey, that job is getting more important, more urgent, all the time.

So on behalf of the writers whose work you're about to encounter, thank you for trusting them with your time. I've already read these stories, several times, and I can assure you: they won't let you down.

Jo Gatford is making a welcome return to our pages here, following her Writer's Award-winning story 'Yellow Rock' in New Ghost Stories IV.

Inside Voices
Jo Gatford

They stop in the middle of Death Valley and crack an egg onto the hood of the car – to see if it'll fry, like the guy in the service station said it would – but it just slides off, leaving a greasy smear in the dusty desert floor.

'Well, that's disappointing,' Nadia says, and her little phrase somehow manages to encompass the entire three weeks. Dan thinks maybe she means it to reach even beyond that.

She sits silent while he drives, knitting a baby blanket for his pregnant sister in curved stripes that undulate like waves over her knees. She turns the A/C up so high it manifests as tinnitus.

'Isn't it a bit hot to be knitting?'

'Do you know how long this is going to take? She's due in October, Daniel.'

He knows not to argue when she uses his name like that. He wonders how big this blanket is going to end up.

It is a necessary hyperfixation. He knows this. But it's as if she starts a new line on purpose every time they're about to leave the hotel room or stop for a bathroom break or do anything other than sit staring at the pile of wool in her lap.

'After this row,' she'll say, and he'll wait, counting the clack of needles, until she's done. One-hundred-and-forty-six stitches per stripe. A complex alternating combination of knits and purls and deliberately slipped stitches that creates a pattern of holes just small enough for baby fingers to poke through.

And when she slides the last loop off the needle she'll sigh, wrap the blanket around the ball of yarn and lay it carefully on the dashboard as if the whole holiday is thoroughly inconveniencing her project.

Her thumbs twitch whenever it isn't in her hands, twisting invisible yarn wherever she goes.

* * *

He fills the cloud with photos. She puts on six pounds in a week. They lose ninety-four dollars in Vegas and watch a small child vomit over the salad bar. Nadia drops a stitch on the I-10 and calls the blanket a cunt.

'Woah,' he says, ghosting the brake in some automatic response to her anger.

She is out of breath, even though she has been sitting in the passenger seat for ninety minutes straight, moving nothing but wrists and fingers and eyeballs and lungs.

'I could just buy her one. She won't care how many hours I've spent on this.'

'I'll tell her how hard you've worked.'

'That would ruin the point.'

What, that you're better than her? he wants to say. But that's not fair. She's made something for all his nieces and nephews — sock monkeys and melted crayon art in the shape of their initials and little crocheted hats that look like strawberries. She dropped off an entire lasagne at the NICU when Molly was born four weeks early. Her thoughtfulness is almost self-punishing. Or perhaps it's an offering, to show whatever gods might be watching that she's got what Pinterest says it takes.

'She should appreciate the effort,' is what he does say.

She bends over the wool to repair her mistake and he doesn't know if the muttered *forfucksake* is for him or his sister or the blanket or herself.

* * *

In Palm Springs they stop at a mall with an indoor ice rink.

'In the desert!' he says, trying to remember if they used to be the kind of people who did spontaneous things, or he just wishes they were.

'Huh.' She doesn't look up. Doesn't want to skate. Instead, she goes to get coffee and browse for lotion to soothe her dry, clawed hands. He waits on a plastic orange bench that looks like a twisted sculpture and watches a crocodile of pre-schoolers trail past, hand in hand, backpacks covered in stickers and dangling keychains. Their teachers herd them along, reminding them to use their inside voices in big, disapproving tones.

When Nadia reappears with three shopping bags but no coffee, he uses his inside voice to ask her to dinner.

She threatens a laugh but doesn't deliver, watching the trail of kids disappear around the corner. 'What are you on about?'

She sits next to him and arranges the bags between her knees. He reaches out to stroke the fine hairs on the back of her neck and she shivers under the air conditioning.

'When I saw you over there I thought, "wow, she's beautiful", and then realised "she" was my wife.'

'I don't know if I'm flattered or worried you've been finding other women beautiful.'

'Not other women. You.'

She flicks his hand away like a mosquito. 'Yeah, but you didn't know that at first.'

* * *

He has this vision of them forty years from now: grey in a distinguished way, a little looser around the middle, a little less bothered about that, wearing whatever their generation will fall back on as retirement clothing — yoga pants, maybe — settled into a quiet routine, orbiting around one another without the need to fill silences. The world has not sunk into catastrophic climate change-induced chaos and they are somehow as comfortably wealthy as their boomer parents. They have a fire pit at the end of the garden. A dog that she has come to love, despite it taking him almost this long to persuade her to get one. They listen to the music they listened to at uni and think it's funny they used to think their own grandparents' music was old fashioned when really it was just their teenage selves imprinting emotion onto vinyl.

He still loves her. He tells her often. And she's stopped replying, 'Well, you're stuck with me,' before she says it back.

* * *

That night they have dinner at a neon diner where each table houses a birdcage full of chirping, shitting budgerigars in yellow and blue and green.

'I mean. That's just unsanitary,' she says.

The first words on the menu are: *Do not feed the birds.*

She pulls out her blanket before they've even ordered and adds a rippling purple row, the twitching ball of wool rolling in the crumbs on the seat beside her. The waiter compliments her on it, calls it 'old school', and she laughs then — loud and fake and wide enough to show her molars.

'It's costing me a fortune in yarn. But it's not for me. It's a gift.'

The waiter nods politely, tumbling his pencil over his knuckles one by one, already fading out.

Nadia stabs at the menu with one blunt needle. 'Fuck it. We should get cocktails.'

'Great!' The waiter reanimates; starts reeling off recommendations.

Dan tries to catch her hand across the table but she props the menu up between them.

'Should you really be...?'

This time her laugh makes a scraping noise. The canaries echo her like a chorus. 'God, it's just one drink, Daniel. Calm down.'

She orders a daiquiri but swaps it for his Coke halfway through. Says everything tastes weird and she feels sick anyway. Pokes a french fry through the bars of the birdcage.

He doesn't say a single one of his thoughts. About the way she was looking at the waiter. About how he must be ten years younger than them. About how ten years ago they would have thought this place was amazing in a terrible, kitsch, public health violation way. About how they used to make jokes about things like this instead of pretending to laugh with strangers.

He worries about the way she talks to him, sometimes. The way she talks about her friends. His sister. How she might talk to a child.

They split dessert — pistachio ice cream the same colour as the latest stripe on the blanket — and he counts the stitches until they can leave.

* * *

He has driven all nine-hundred-and-forty-three miles they've covered so far, but she still tells him when to change lanes and when he's going too fast and when he should have checked his mirrors.

She gets tired easily. Irritated even easier. He is as understanding as he can be. It's still early days and they've made a silent agreement not to talk about it. Or, at least, he's too afraid to bring it up unless she does. But the whole trip is a reminder. They'd booked it in another 'fuck it' moment. A mourning consolation. A flipside distraction. They hadn't even been trying, this time. But then, three days before their flight — two lines.

'That's how it happens sometimes,' his sister said. 'Like your body knows when you've stopped stressing about it. You know, how cats always sit on the people who don't make a fuss of them.'

He didn't pass that particular piece of wisdom on to Nadia. She didn't seem to be able to speak about it all — as if she were trying to swallow a boulder whole.

'It's not real until the scan,' she said, and so it wasn't allowed to be real for him either.

The appointment isn't for another three weeks after they get back. Another three weeks of treading water, a frayed line stretching between them, focusing so hard on staying above the surface that they have no breath left to call out to each other.

She started the blanket on the plane; said she didn't want to spend twelve hours watching shitty movies, but ended up looking over his shoulder anyway, asking, 'Who's that?' or 'What did they just say?' every few minutes. He watched the stripes form beneath her fingers — a wavering, disordered rainbow — and whispered the actors' lines back to her without complaint. He could do these small things for her. Because he could not promise her anything else.

* * *

In San Diego she gets sunstroke and they spend three days in the hotel room. The TV is as wide as the wardrobe it sits in. There's a whole movie category called 'old skool' and they watch *Forrest Gump* and *Groundhog Day* and eat Pringles out of the mini bar. Nadia switches to yellow yarn and quotes all the lines she knows without even looking up.

On the third night, she discovers a tiny red scorpion in the bathroom. It's two inches long and doesn't do much but run in circles, disoriented by her stampeding feet. He traps it under a little plastic trash can and beats it to death with a complimentary shrink-wrapped slipper. She won't step on the floor again that night but thanks him over and over again and kisses his neck as if she might go further, but then she puts the TV back on and makes him watch *Miss Congeniality 2*.

She wakes him in the early jet lag hours to say she can't stop thinking: 'If that was the baby, where's the mummy scorpion?'

He laughs, to turn the fear into the kind of mock outrage she finds easier to process, but when he turns on the light her face is wet and he's never known what to do with that.

She cries for a while, quiet and deep, until his chest is slick with saline and snot. She lies in it anyway and the side of her face sticks to him.

'Do you want to watch another movie?' he says. He can do these small things, even though they're not enough. She rocks her head in the negative, peels her face away and sits up, pulling her knitting onto her lap.

'You can go back to sleep,' she tells him, and it is an order — her way of relieving him from duty, perhaps. Cutting the string between the tin cans.

Three weeks until he gets her back, one way or the other. He is trying to understand — to respect the fact that he will never understand — but he is scared, too. Of how changed they have already become. How different they might end up.

Her mouth becomes a line as her eyes focus on the stitches, and he has become so used to this expression that he finds it hard to remember what she looked like before she carried worry around like a shawl.

He rolls away and pretends to be unconscious, watching the carpet for mummy scorpions.

* * *

They're back on the road the next day. Final leg. One last push. Making memories. The dream trip. Almost over. Thank fuck.

The smell of the fake leather upholstery has begun to make him nauseous. The feel of wool on his skin makes him clench. He has to move the blanket from every single chair he tries to sit in, like some cocky alpha cat. It spills across her lap and into the footwell of the passenger seat. His hand brushes against it whenever he releases the handbrake.

'I think it's nearly done,' she says, knotting off another row, switching from purple to red. Her sigh sounds like it came up from the bottom of a well and he wonders if she's as sick of the sight of stripes as he is.

'It's amazing,' is what he does say. And it is. It is art. An impossibly tangible thing made from nothing but twisted string. She has shown him how to frog a row in one swift pull – ten minutes of labour unravelled in a moment. He's watched her dismantle lines at a time because of one erroneous stitch. She has always been patient. Determined. To a frightening degree. He has always enjoyed being afraid of her in that way. A religious kind of awe. The knowledge that she will do the impossible for you, if she decides to. If she chooses you. And perhaps that's why her uncertainty is so unbearable.

She looks across at him for the first time in hours and her leading question feels genuine. 'Do you think she'll like it?'

'She'll love it,' he obliges, willingly, even though he knows it's not enough. His sister will make it a big deal and Nadia will try to make it into nothing, as if it hasn't consumed the last three weeks of their lives. She has always needed to prove some floating, indistinct point to his family – incapable of believing that they might be kind and welcoming and generous because they actually just like her. That they want him to be happy and they trust in his judgement. That she deserves it.

She makes a scrunched up face but he needs her to know, to believe him, and he squeezes her leg through the blanket. 'She's going to be so grateful, Nad.'

She rolls her eyes at the nickname – Nad and Dan, human palindromes – one of their first stupid jokes. He'd wanted it printed on a banner for the wedding but she'd vetoed it, said it made them sound like puppets on a kid's show, as if getting married suddenly meant they couldn't be idiots anymore.

She pulls the blanket out from under his hand, rolls it up around the skein and holds it to her sternum.

They haven't told anyone yet. 'Don't want to steal your sister's thunder,' she'd said. 'At least not until after the scan.' If they get that far.

But he's known it's been coming. Feels the tension in every stitch. The regret that she only learnt to knit afterwards: a hobby to keep her mind off it.

They hadn't named the others. One, a clump of cells, Two, a smudged heartbeat. 'Third time's the charm,' his mother had said after that one, and Nadia hasn't really spoken to her since.

He forces himself to move his palm from her leg to the bundle of wool in her arms and squeezes that instead.

'I never made them anything,' she says.

He wants to say, 'You didn't need to. You don't need to,' but he can't drive when she's crying so he says nothing, shifts his hand back onto the wheel and pulls into the outer lane.

* * *

By the time they get to San Francisco the blanket is absurdly long, entirely out of proportion to its width — big enough to wrap up triplets — but the first thing she does after check-in is google craft shops.

They forego the bridge and the wharf and Alcatraz and visit a store in the mission district with hanging crochet birds in the window. He waits out on the street. The proximity to so much yarn makes him itch just thinking about it.

Inside, Nadia brings out her creation and becomes the nucleus at the centre of a clustered cell of women who admire her zigzag waves, her regimented pattern, her careful colour choices. They run their fingers over the dizzying stripes and stretch them out to their full length. She is illuminated in their appreciation but her smile is fixed and performative. He wants to ask her to stop. He wants to take the loose end and yank it. To feel the snap of each stitch as it comes free. He wants her to look him in the eye and tell him if this is what she really wants. If he is what she wants. But he is almost afraid of touching her. Afraid of what her answer might be.

These women don't even know her, but something has shifted inside the room and now they are pulling her close, tucking her into their shoulders, stroking her hair, and she is crying again – he can hear it through the glass, though he cannot understand what she's telling them in between breaths – and they are nodding, all of them, as if they have been waiting for her to arrive here, today, right this minute, and one of them carefully takes the blanket out of her hands and out of sight and the rest of them pull in closer like the neck of a drawstring bag, holding her up in the middle of the circle.

* * *

When she comes back outside her face is red and tender. She presses her forehead into his chest and breathes out for so long it feels like she's deflating. She is carrying something in a brown paper bag, but it is far too small to be the blanket. Before he can ask where it is, one of the women from the store appears inside the window display, beneath the crochet birds, threading Nadia's masterpiece onto a curtain pole.

It reaches all the way to the floor and the stripes sway as it settles. Sunlight seeps through the holes between the stitches, speckling the wall behind. He has not seen it like this before, at its fullest. He can pick out every turn of her wrist, every swear word, every hunch-backed sigh, and it is vast and intricate and perfect. The unfinished end is still attached to a ball of burgundy wool, unspooling itself towards the glass with each soft sweep. Nadia keeps her eyes closed, breathing faster than she needs to, fingers chain-linked at the small of his back. She is all bone and pinched muscle, but has always fitted right here beneath his chin, no matter what shape she is, so perfectly he half-expects to hear a 'click' when they come together.

The woman in the window steps back and admires the display with one decisive nod, then looks up past the blanket and right at him, and her, and them, for a long, open second.

From here, he can see down into the paper bag at Nadia's feet. Inside is a single skein of yarn, multiple shades blending one into another, yard upon yard. A small, complicated thing, twisted in on itself and wrapped with tissue.

* * *

Six hours into the flight home, his phone pings a notification as she adds the scan date to his calendar.

It's not real for another three weeks but it's something. A digital dot.

He looks sideways at her but she's pretending to watch a movie. The paper bag is still between her knees. He nudges it with his foot and it crinkles.

'Are you going to start a new one?' he asks her.

She doesn't take off her headphones. Maybe doesn't even hear him. But she lets him weave his fingers in and out of hers.

The second of our two Fiction Desk regulars featured in this volume, Alastair Chisholm once again sets aside his writing for children, and gives the adults something to think about.

Mayflies
Alastair Chisholm

She sits at the end of the bar, half hidden in shadows that separate her from the other patrons, drinking dark smoky whisky from a short glass. Somehow, he knows it's whisky, just as he knew she would be here tonight. It's always whisky. She's always here.

He shakes the raindrops from his hat and turns his collar back down, removes his coat, glances around. It's a typical evening, not busy, not quiet. He recognises an old man in the far corner, a regular, sitting with a pint and the sports pages. On his left, a group of women have camped at two tables. They're shrieking with laughter and banging shot glasses on the table, and cheering at one in the middle wearing a plastic-gold crown. He flinches slightly as he passes them, but they ignore him. He reaches the end of the bar and sits next to the woman.

She doesn't react. She sits perfectly still, arms resting lightly against the edge of the counter, both hands around her glass, gazing ahead as if considering herself in the mirror behind the bar. She is wearing a black dress and a gold necklace; on her left wrist a row of golden bracelets glimmer against her warm, brown skin. Black hair, thick but not long, held in a clasp just above her neck.

The bartender comes across and nods towards him, and he orders a vodka and Coke. The man prefers whisky: he likes the golden light and the taste of grass fire. But vodka is safer, easier to conceal. He takes a sip, closes his eyes. The hen party shrieks again, but muted now; not quieter, but somehow further away, as if the shadows around the two of them form a curtain.

'I miss the days when you could smoke,' he says at last.

She says nothing. She blinks, slowly, and sips at her drink. The scent from her glass is salty, almost tar-like, and too strong for him – Laphroaig, perhaps, or Lagavulin. He steals a glimpse at her face, sees mascara smeared under one eye, imperfectly corrected, and the slow pulse on her neck.

'I mean, when you could smoke in these places. Gave you something to do, you know? With your hands. I miss it.' He turns towards her. 'My name's William.'

As if she has been waiting for her cue, she sighs and turns and looks at him.

'William.' Her voice is low, well spoken, with an accent he can't place. Her eyes are the same colour as her drink, dark and deep. 'That's an old name.'

William thinks about this. 'I'm old, I suppose,' he replies. 'Old enough to remember when this was real.' He shakes his head. 'And you are?'

One corner of her mouth lifts. She holds his look until he thinks she isn't going to answer, and then purses her lips in a *why-not* gesture. 'Nadia.'

He smiles. 'Pleased to meet you, Nadia.'

He lifts his glass and she hers, tilting it towards his but not letting them touch.

'I don't smoke,' she says.

'No. Me neither, these days.'

'What did you mean, "When this was real"?'

William looks around. The room is long, the bar running up the length of one side like an old American saloon. Aged but well looked after, in polished wood and low lights, and an old-fashioned mirror behind the bottles at the back. Old music plays softly in the background. The hen party is debating, he notices; some of them want to move on, some want to stay. One girl, at the edge of the group, sits quietly and stares at her drink with an expression of dismay.

'This place,' he says. 'When it was real before, you know? Like this.' He taps the bar top, solid wood, stained and damaged and mended and polished. 'This isn't real. Five years ago, this was a nightclub, neon and black plastic, and the bar was at the back wall there. It was a proper drinking dive once, a rough old place. It's been a disco, a coffee shop ...' He taps the wood again. 'They ripped this all out, then put it all back in. It's fake. I mean, it's real, but it's not *real*.'

He looks up at her. 'Some things are real and not real, you know?'

She takes another sip of her drink.

'Do you come here often?' he asks, and winces at the cliché. But she shrugs.

'Sometimes. When I need to.' She raises an eyebrow. 'I remember when it was the disco.'

'You don't seem old enough.'

'Mmm.' She smiles, as if to herself, and finishes her whisky.

'Would you like a drink?' she asks.

* * *

They talk, as the evening settles around them. The hen party orders a round of cocktails with outrageous names, hooting in raucous glee as they arrive decorated with sparklers in suggestive shapes. There are others around, too, at tables, or leaning against the bar; but not at the end where William and Nadia sit, pooled in darkness and soft endless calm.

'It's always the same,' she says, watching the others. 'Have you noticed?'

He frowns. 'Same as what?'

'Same as always. The place changes, the people. But it's always the same. The conversations, the jokes, the dramas. It's a pattern, repeated. The same moves. The same dance.'

'I ... suppose so,' he says.

Her eyes flick back to his face, dark.

'What do you do, William?'

'I work in shipping,' he says. He likes the sound of that. But then he hesitates. 'I mean ... logistics for shipping. I mean, in the logistics department.' He gives a crooked grin. 'I move paper around and sign things. It's not important.'

She shrugs. 'It's important. You make things happen. Without you, everything would stop.'

He can't tell if she's laughing at him, but she raises her glass and drinks, and he does the same. He tries to think of something to say. He wants to ask her if she's married, but it seems crass.

'Are you married?' she asks. She runs a forefinger around the rim of her glass, watching it as if uninterested in his answer.

'I, ah. Yes. I mean ...' He frowns. 'I mean, I was. Not anymore. You?'

'Yes,' she says.

'Ah.'

Her face twists into a wry expression. 'Always the same moves,' she says, and he smiles as he understands.

'Always the same dance,' he replies.

* * *

'He's a good man, in his way. He provided for us: arranged for us to come here, to safety; looked after us when we arrived. We had lost everything, but he gave my father a job, my brothers ...'

'Do you love him?'

She stares into her glass. 'No,' she says. 'Not ever. I tried ... I come here to escape, for a while. To see people. To ... feel something.'

She blinks, twice, looks away. When she turns back, her voice is soft. 'What about you? Why are you here, William?'

He shrugs. 'Old times' sake, I suppose,' he says. 'I was walking past, thought I'd look in. I used to drink here.'

'When you were married?'

Now it's his turn to smile sadly, to look down.

'Yes.' And then, without knowing why, he tells her everything. About a boring, unfulfilled life in an office, counting out days. About a woman who came into that life; beautiful, bright, and far, far above what he had any right to expect. About happiness; about the way she looked at him; first with love, then with confusion ...

Then with disappointment.

'When Peggy was born, I thought it would be ... something, you know?' he says. 'Something to bring us back, the same old story. But money was tight, and I couldn't, I wasn't ... good enough. Her parents lent us some, her father, he told me ...' He grimaces.

'I started coming here after work. Once, twice. Then every night. She thought I was working late, repaying ... I couldn't face her. Every night —'

He swallows the last of his vodka in a sudden, vicious move, swings his head around to the bartender, waves his empty glass.

'But she's not waiting for you anymore,' she murmurs.

He notices that for the first time one hand has uncurled from around her glass. It reaches, not quite towards him, but to a space near him; to the world between them, where for a moment he knows that, if he wanted, he could put his own hand. It's an unconscious gesture, casual and unimportant. He could just move his hand ...

He sits up a little and leans away.

'She left, of course,' he says. 'Went back to her parents, took Peggy. I haven't seen her since.' He blinks. 'I'm sorry, I don't know why I'm telling you this. I don't ...'

She gazes at him, her eyes dark, and he shakes his head.

'I'm sorry.'

Glasses chink, and conversations echo around them.

'I am sorry for your pain,' she says.

He looks away, to the end of the bar. Then he frowns in surprise.

'Hey,' he says, 'I know him.' Halfway along the bar a group of men are drinking. One leans against the counter, the others stand, and the scene is like courtiers listening to their king. The leaning man is broad shouldered in a leather jacket, black haired, turned slightly away from William so that his face is hidden, but the pose and confidence of his stance are immediately familiar. He's talking, waving his glass slightly for emphasis, telling a story to his audience.

'Jimmy something,' mutters William. 'Used to come in here, oh, years ago. He's a foreman at the docks, bit of a big man. I remember him and old Ray Haddon squared up once, he ...'

The man turns, and William stops. Same hair, but a different nose, long and straight where Jimmy's was flared, and his chin pointed where Jimmy's was square.

'Huh.'

'He's not your friend?'

William shrugs to cover his embarrassment. 'He seemed just the same. You know, the way he stood, the others.'

'He's a pattern,' she says. 'Just patterns, over and over.'

William chews the inside of his cheek, looks down into his glass. The man who is not Jimmy finishes his story, and the others laugh on cue just as William remembers, dutiful and pleasing, and the big man finishes his drink and hands some notes to the barman for another round. William looks towards the old man in the corner, the one he'd thought he recognised, and realises he was wrong about him, too: the person he remembered had a moustache, thick and white; this one is clean shaven.

'And us,' murmurs Nadia, and William starts.

'What?'

'Strangers at the bar, with a past? Aren't we the same? Patterns, over and over, and over ...'

William has the curious feeling that something is about to happen. He doesn't know what to say; it's as if his lines have been repeated too many times before, by different actors in the same role. He hesitates, feeling the bar noise fade to silence.

When he lifts his head, Nadia is looking away, towards the hen party and the girl at the edge, who is weeping. Of course, he thinks, as if from far away. There's always a Crying Girl. They watch as the girl stands abruptly and walks away from the group, her arms crossed tight around her body. She is trembling. She walks towards them, looking up at them as she nears, and her face shows a look of faint recognition as she sees Nadia ...

... and she stumbles through them and beyond.

'What the *hell* — ?'

William tries to leap backwards and as the girl passes through them, clothes and soft pale skin and grey misery in a wash of horror and terror, and beyond, through him and through the counter too. She turns just before the mirror and one hand reaches out as if to push open a door, a door that doesn't exist but just for a moment he remembers a doorway there, sees something —

— and she is gone.

Nadia watches the space where the girl disappeared. Her face is calm, her skin shimmers in their dim-lit corner. She sips at her whisky, and for the first time William allows himself to see her, to really *see* her; and the wall behind her, and through her. She faces him, unconcerned.

He turns away and lifts his glass with a shaking hand, feeling it rattle against his teeth as he drinks. He finishes it, sucks at the dregs, puts it back down with a clatter. His lips suddenly seem very dry and he finds it hard to swallow.

He knows she's waiting for him to speak. He doesn't look up. The old man from the corner comes to the bar, chats to the barman, orders another pint of ale in a dimpled pint glass.

After a long time, William says, in a hoarse, low voice, 'I've seen you before.'

She waits.

He says, 'When I used to come here every night. I saw you at the end of the bar, like you are now.'

She doesn't answer him directly. Instead, she says: 'I wanted to feel something. I ached for it. Our old lives were gone, my friends were dead, this country was cold and small and my husband ... I just wanted to feel *something*.'

Her bracelets clink against the counter as she speaks. There is a long, twisting line up the inside of her wrist, pale and torn.

'What am I, then?' she asks. 'What am I, in this place?'

'I don't ... I don't understand,' he whispers.

'Yes, you do. You see us.'

She leans towards him, and the scent of her perfume is candlewax and rain and red wine and shadows. 'We are all patterns, William. The living, the dead, we're all the same. What am I, over and over? The Woman With A Past? The Femme Fatale? And you, the Haunted Man? Over and over. Over ... and *over*.'

William shivers. He wishes there was more drink in his glass. He's still holding it, empty, on the counter; it rattles against the wood as his hands shake. Old man's hands, old and palsied, red at the knuckles, shaking from fear or too many vodkas, and Margaret at home waiting for him to prove himself, to be someone he could never be, every day, while he hid here, the Failure, over and over ...

'You knew I would be here,' she whispers. 'You came here to find me.'

He sighs.

'Every night, you come here.'

'What?' He frowns. 'No. No, just ... Just this evening ...'

'Every night, William. Over and over.'

'N-no ...'

'This is how it goes,' she says. 'The strangers meet. They talk, they nearly connect. But wrapped in their own misery, they leave, alone, into the night. Over and over ...'

She rests one hand next to his, palm downwards.

'... But they don't *have* to.'

He doesn't understand, but he feels her presence, so close. All he has to do is touch her. His own hand drifts until it hovers just above hers, trembling.

'It's all I have,' he whispers.

Her eyes glow. Her skin glows. She is so *alive*.

'They're waiting at home,' he tries. 'She loves me. I have to get back.'

'She's long gone, William. She's a ghost.'

'I'm ... I'm scared.'

'You don't have to be.' She is still smiling, but her eyes are full of whisky smoke; beguiling, beseeching. 'We could end it, William. You don't have to keep doing this. We don't have to. We could be *free*.'

But he shakes his head again. 'No. *No!*'

He stands suddenly and backs away from the bar, ignoring the other drinkers.

'I have to *go*,' he says, and staggers away, out into the night, away, away.

She doesn't stop him. She watches as he leaves, still smiling; and then she turns back and examines herself in the mirror. After a while, her smile falters, and her head drops.

* * *

He comes again, the following evening. She observes him in the mirror as he removes his hat and shakes it, takes off his old-fashioned coat, glances around.

He walks towards her through the crowd, ignoring them. They don't notice him. They don't feel the raindrops that fall from his coat; they don't see him as he drifts, through people, through chairs.

He sits next to her and she studies his face in the mirror, grey with worry and failure, mottled with burst blood vessels, lost. Bar lights shine faintly through him. A shadow appears behind the counter and he looks up. He says something, and the shadow moves away and returns with a hollow, thin echo of a glass, which he lifts with trembling care. He drinks, puts the glass down, makes some comment. She ignores it and waits, and eventually he turns to her.

'My name's William,' he says.

She sighs, and turns on her cue.

'William,' she says. 'That's an old name.'

David Malvina's story first came to us in response to our themed call for stories about books. For all the smoke and flames, it's a chilling reminder of the horrors of redundancy.

Book Burning
David Malvina

He led a troop of six people and they went from house to house taking the books and burning them as they went along. The burning was done with no publicity, and the fires were extinguished as soon as the books could not be rescued. As soon as they could no longer be read, or their pictures studied, they put the flames out and moved on. Often when they reached open fields they would take off their guns and collapse out of pleasure and exhaustion. All of them had been chosen for the delicacy of their feelings. Frequently they were overwhelmed by the number of people they helped in just one single day.

It was going to be a normal day and they started early. They pulled themselves up from the earth and grass. Sometimes there were things planted in the fields, although nothing they recognised from the books. At the first house most of these books looked as if they'd never been used. They had been read, but there were no marks or stains on them, and there were none of the little notes or bookmarks that were so common. The dust jackets went up first, with a pink flame that was characteristic of books of a certain age and the materials used in their production. Next the glossy surface of the hard covers would peel and split, racing to the corners, blisters would form on the white cardboard, and sometimes the remains of the laminate would seem to boil like a liquid in tiny pools that rose and sank. They had learnt to use a precise language when they observed these things, perhaps a habit they'd absorbed from the books themselves. After all they loved them just as much as the people relinquishing them or actively piling them into their arms.

Among their equipment was a set of replacement books which the people in every house were always invited to inspect and to choose from if they wished. If they had time they would even erect a little portable stand to display the books, and leave this on show at a suitable distance from the fire. As the old books were piled onto the flames, they would encourage the dazed residents to look at all the titles which had been chosen so carefully, and which thousands of other people had already found to be helpful. The most popular book, or at least the one they promoted more actively than any other at the moment, was a large format book called *Do You Know All About the Stars?* It had lots of great pictures but of course the point was to look up from the pictures. Today at the first house a mother and her three children looked through all the books and then chose *Do You Know All About the Stars?*, and once the fire had been put out (the family did this — he encouraged the children to have fun with the buckets of water), the new book was taken inside, two of the children holding it together between them like something they'd adopted. The family continued to watch them from the kitchen window as they packed up and then consulted their lists.

At the second house the owner, who lived by himself, refused to listen and closed the door on them, and so they waited and made sure that he could see them and after no more than five minutes he rushed out and dumped an enormous heap of books onto the fire, which they'd already lit. Then he rushed inside, his white hair blowing in all directions, and came back with three more stacks of books which he threw down onto the flames with too much force. As they tidied the fire he was invited to look at the replacement books, and he asked if he could have three copies of *Do You Know All About the Stars?* A master copy, another one in case he should ever mislay the first, and a third copy so that he could pass it on to someone else. He was certain he'd want to do this and he said he could hardly wait. Three copies were handed over and he took them inside with great ceremony while they tended the flames. He did not emerge again.

The books that concerned the little troop were mixed up indiscriminately with any number of other things, and their leader tried to identify as many of them as he could before the covers were burnt. Slender volumes of poetry burnt alongside books on French and Italian food. A ten volume encyclopaedia of music went up beside novels with garish covers, some with flames in the pictures, three dictionaries of the sort which translated between different languages, more books about Italian food, books on psychology and philosophy, and a huge atlas of the world in a thick cardboard case which burnt very slowly. The picture of the globe on the outside of this thick case stood up among the flames until something shifted underneath it. Then it was the turn of a book about the great gardens of the world to lie on the top.

It was all quite straightforward at the next two houses. The people at the first house argued with them but then argued among themselves and then gathered all the books and looked at each one in turn before they put them on the fire. There was an enormous variety in this hoard. He looked through one of them himself, a thick book with pictures not only of each recipe, but between each section as well. There was also a kind of dictionary of ingredients with little pictures of each one displayed on a dark wooden surface. Light was reflected from this wooden surface as well as from the polished skins of red peppers, purple aubergines, and long fat green beans, and from tidy heaps of beans of every colour and shape, and even from small mounds of rock salt, which appeared in more than one place and had a pinkish tinge.

He turned through the pages. Roasted red and golden beetroot, roast potatoes and Jerusalem artichokes with lemon and sage. Butterbeans with sweet chilli sauce and fresh herbs. Roast chicken with sumac and lemon, marinated rack of lamb with coriander and honey, fried scallops with asparagus. A green olive loaf, small brown rolls, and loaves shaped like knots with a shiny crust and little seeds scattered on the crust. Lentils with mushrooms and sweet spices, corn and spring onion pancakes, aubergines with tomatoes and roasted garlic. Chicken with roast onion and thyme gravy, a potato salad with lemon and spinach, and pasta with spicy sausage, basil and mustard. In the same book there was also a section about cheese which began with a picture of all the different kinds arranged together on a marble surface.

The next house was a big place behind gates and they were led to the kitchen and left to gather all the books themselves while the owners went off and waited somewhere else. The kitchen had its own door and they made the fire on some flagstones just a few metres from the door.

One of the books was lying open on the table, right there. He looked through it while the others were taken outside. A

Karahi chicken dish with fresh herbs and spiced rotis, cumin paprika wedges, and tiger prawns in lime, ginger and mustard. Lamb masala using cinnamon sticks, cardamom, fresh chilli, and pomegranate seeds. Roasted vegetable biryani, an aubergine salad with chickpeas and tamarind, and a lentil salad with toasted cumin. Spiced vegetable soup with roasted chilli, tomato and red onion salad with roasted coriander, and flatbreads cooked with chopped garlic and ginger. Pickles made with preserved lemon, or with tomatoes and chillies or with mangoes.

It went on the fire and once it began to burn they put the fire out and moved on. It was an hour before they reached the next house and here something unusual happened, as no one was there but the door was open and it was easy to find the books. They stood in the small kitchen for a while. They ate something and waited for another hour then took all the books outside and burnt them.

Fish soup using four kinds of fish, grilled marinated lamb, baked goat's cheese in pastry, and a mushroom risotto made with leeks, parsley and garlic. Avocado salad, stuffed red peppers using thyme, garlic and anchovies, and pastries filled with chopped mushrooms and different cheeses. Lasagne, sausage carbonara, and recipes for pizza dough. A peppery beef stew, a summer vegetable terrine, a spicy winter casserole made using cauliflower, and a mushroom and cheese omelette with salad and fried potatoes.

Frangipane tart, raspberry cheesecake, and shortbread. Pies made with blue cheese, or with smoked chicken, or with roasted vegetables. A tart made with smoked salmon and asparagus, cottage pie with cheese in the potato mash, macaroni cheese, corned beef hash, tarka dhal, and fried rice. Lentil and bacon soup, curried parsnip soup, tomato soup, goulash, spicy sweet potato soup and onion soup, rich and dark. Recipes for focaccia, for ciabatta, for rye bread and soda bread, for white tin loaf and brown rolls.

In all the books he examined at this house there were lines crossing through the pages from corner to corner, lines and scribbles through the lists of ingredients. He'd seen this before. As you couldn't get almost all the things in these books any more there were hardly any pages left without these scribbles and lines.

To reach the next house they had to leave the road and go down a long path. It was a small place, neat as a doll's house, with lattice windows and flower boxes underneath them. It had trees on all sides and there was smoke coming from the chimney. After they were shown all the books the others took them outside and started the fire. He stayed in the kitchen with the woman who lived there while she found a few more books that were stuck in odd places by themselves.

He stood there while she found them and placed them on the table one by one.

The third one she found had an enormous close-up picture of a slice of cake on its front cover, a lemon sponge cake with two layers of icing and little pieces of crystallised sugar.

'I know this book,' he said. He didn't mean he'd seen it in another of the houses they'd visited, but she didn't ask him what he meant.

The picture on the cover was so close to the cake you could see the texture and how it was dense and had a faint shine because it was so rich with all the sugar and fat. There were some loose crumbs beneath the lower edge of the slice and these had a faint shine as well.

She had brought him a chair and he took it and sat down.

'Thank you,' he said.

Lemon cake, iced cupcakes, sultana cake, treacle tart and chocolate brownies. Apple and cinnamon tarts, these ones shown on a tray held by someone's hands wearing blue gloves. Scones, two different kinds, piled up on plates that had pink flowers around the edge and gold rims. Double chocolate chip cookies, baked lime cheesecake, almond biscuits, white chocolate and raspberry biscuits, and sticky ginger cake. Apple pie, apple crumble, and Victoria sponge with icing and jam. Mince pies, Christmas cake, and a special chocolate cake 'for New Year's Day'.

Eva Carson is making her first Fiction Desk appearance with this beautifully observed story that explores mysteries both supernatural and social.

The Business at Tradeston

Eva Carson

I first met Andrew Paterson in a pub in Tradeston. Paterson was in his early sixties by then, a big man with the solid, heavy build of someone who's spent decades in a job requiring physical labour. I was only twenty, and looked like what I was: a skinny, bookish young man from England, a student at the university.

The pub was the kind of place that often shines out of the grey murk of post-industrial cities like Glasgow: flat roof, damp roughcast walls, steel grilles on the windows, coloured lights in the glass from the gambling machines within. It was, it's safe to say, not the typical student haunt, not even in Glasgow in the early 2000s. The day I met Paterson I was there recklessly, foolishly, on an eccentric little quest to uncover something spooky about the city I'd fallen in love with and decided to make my home.

My quest had been interrupted by a sudden burst of Scottish rain. I'd gone to the pub for shelter and to work out how to get back to the university by bus. It was the late afternoon. Inside the pub, it stank of stale beer and was loud with men and the rattle of the machines. I dripped rainwater on the carpet. The barman was small and wiry, in his forties, and wearing that look I'd come to know well in Glasgow: aggressively quizzical, calmly amused that at any minute things might be about to kick off. He appraised me instantly. He told me I was lost.

'I'm doing research,' I said, and a frown established itself on his face. 'On Glasgow. The landscape. I'm a student.'

He didn't feel the need to respond to this.

'I wondered if you knew where to get the bus,' I said. 'Back to the university.'

'To the university.'

'Yes. The University of Glasgow.'

'The University of Glasgow.'

'It's the 44 to the university,' another voice said. A man had put his elbows on the bar. His biceps stretched the cloth of his T-shirt. There was a pale network of scars across his cheek and over the brow of his left eye. He explained where to get the bus – it was only two streets away and it was an hour till the next one.

There seemed, among the large and variously dangerous-looking men in the place, to have been a collective decision to leave me in peace, so I decided to settle where I was, at the bar, with a pint. I took a moment to look over my papers to see if any of them were dry. They were not.

I was studying for a degree in history. But alongside that, I had a personal project of collecting any weird and spooky stories to do with the city. It was a passion of mine: the usual academic's fantasy that the dusty old papers we comb through might point to something magical, thrilling, and strange. In my first couple of years in the city, I hadn't found much of interest beyond the usual stories told to tourists, but I'd just recently found a very odd account to do with Tradeston.

Tradeston lies just south of the river in Glasgow. Trains coming into the city from the south rumble over it on the bridges, creaking and clanking their way towards the vast old mouth of Central Station. Back then Tradeston was a wasteland of derelict brick factories, ruined Victorian sandstones, and empty warehouses. There were weeds growing on the iron fire escapes, and windows with little else but jagged glass in the sockets of their frames. And there were the blue tin roofs of modern industrial estates, scratching out a living among the remnants of a much older, even ancient place.

Half a mile south of the city centre, in Scotland's biggest city: in any other place, the area would have been transformed into a gleaming redevelopment project. That had happened by then along other stretches of the Clyde, but it had not happened in Tradeston. I decided this marked it out as strange and wanted to investigate.

The main city archives are held in the Mitchell Library, in an extension built in the 1970s. I don't believe it has been redecorated since. I'd grown delirious from the lacquered panels and orange carpets before I found any reward for my curiosity. I'd gone to the dustiest section of the municipal archives, and deliberately to the commercial activity section, as I knew that was most likely to contain any information relating to Tradeston. Within that modest subcategory, I discovered a miscellaneous section, which consisted of a dismaying number of box files. They were of the kind that exists in all such archives: surviving only because no one person has either the authority to dispose of them or the inclination to form a committee to do so. In one of those box files, I found the notebook.

It was inside a file that contained early drafts of what looked like an abandoned redevelopment project for the Tradeston area from the early 1970s. Any historian will tell you that the seventies were vividly haunted by dreams of the utopian future — it was perhaps the last period before all such dreams looked painfully naive. Glasgow dreamed of motorways and high rises, hanging gardens and all mod cons. But in that same decade, the government put the city into a deliberate decline and would pursue a policy of dismantling its industries and communities for the next twenty years. Tradeston hadn't been the city's only wasteland back then.

The notebook was no bigger than the palm of my hand. It was much older than the rest of that section of the archive. Its handwritten entries, meticulously dated, ran from 1842 to 1846, and filled about half the book.

The entries were brief fragments — hand-copied lines from news reports of disappearances and a few lines that I took to be notes from conversations, gossip, and rumours on strange occurrences, superstitions, and even one prophetic dream about a death. But the last entry, which was also the longest entry, was different. It had an effortful quality to it — the writer was not naturally gifted and had strained his or her pen to get the matter down as well as they could.

> *The death of Miss Agnes McMillan of 64 Carswell Street. She lay several days insensible in the Infirmary. But several persons claim to have seen her walking in the city during that time. I heard it from Margaret and from the ladies at the laundry.*
>
> *And when she passed they say there was a figure climbing up the Glasgow Royal Infirmary wall to the window of the ward. There was a single nurse with her*

> who saw it come in to her. I have not got the name of the nurse. She saw the soul return and lie down into the body at the point of death.

On the page opposite this written account was a very rough hand-drawn map of a few streets and their corners. The streets were not labelled except for the part labelled *Carswell Street*. At the bottom of the page, in small capital letters, was the word TRADESTON.

I made enquiries at the desk, of course, and was told the box was merely recorded as a legacy of council restructuring, with no specific contents itemised in the brief description.

I took the notebook to the library's copier room and held the pages open against the glass. Then I put it back in the box file.

There is no Carswell Street on any map of Glasgow. The day I met Paterson, I'd gone down to Tradeston to see if I could spot an old street layout or any other clue as to where it might have been. In practice, this basically looked like me wandering into workers' yards in Glasgow and asking questions, in an area that I later learned was becoming notorious for organised crime. It was probably just as well the rain put a stop to my explorations.

The photocopies of the notebook, when I drew them from my pocket in the pub, were now damp little packets that came apart gently when I unfolded them onto the bar.

Silly dreams. Superstition, gossip, and anecdote. A curious doodle of a map. Walking into the pub had given me a different perspective. I felt silly, like a foolish boy among men. Cities, villages, the wilderness — really all places belonged to men like these, living lives and not scraping about in strange little stories of the past. I felt stupid.

> *...There was a single nurse with her who saw it come in to her. I have not got the name of the nurse. She saw the soul return and lie down into the body at the point of death.*

Gradually, I became aware that someone was reading over my shoulder. The space next to me at the bar had now been filled by a man in his sixties, tall and broad shouldered, wearing an orange hi-vis jacket spattered with rain. When I looked up into his face, I saw he wore an expression of total absorption. I let him carry on his study, waiting awkwardly for the barman to set down his pint and break the spell.

But when the barman set the pint down, nothing changed. After an age had passed, the man spoke.

'Where did you get these?'

'I'm a student,' I said. 'At the university. I'm interested in the landscape and folklore? The history of the city?'

'I see. And these are from the university. They keep things like that there.'

'No, these are from the Mitchell Library. There's an old council archive. These are just copies,' I said. I laughed. 'Luckily, given the rain!'

He didn't smile. He'd placed his hand on the bar, on the papers, as if to weigh them down and keep them in place.

'And what are they for?'

I told him I'd hoped to spot traces of the old street layout. 'But I haven't found anything. Maybe there's nothing left.'

'So you took this for a true account?'

I blushed and stammered something about social history and belief systems. I expected him to make some dry Glaswegian comment, but instead he just said he didn't think I'd find what I was looking for.

'Ah, yes,' I said. 'Quite possibly not.'

He gathered the papers into his fist and squashed them into a rain-sodden ball of mulch on the countertop. The barman was passing with his cloth and swept it up into the bin.

* * *

The following morning, I visited the Mitchell again for some work I had to do as part of my degree. I planned to make new photocopies from the notebook. I admit I was also trying to work up the courage to steal it.

I'd been working on a university essay for a couple of hours when I caught a glimpse of the man from Tradeston. He was in jeans and a brown jacket instead of his orange hi-vis, but I recognised him straight away. He was walking slowly along the shelves of box files in the archive, his head bowed, his hands in his pockets. I was confident he wouldn't have the faintest idea where to start. There were at least fifty boxes of the old council papers, and the notebook wasn't itemised anywhere. I watched him speak to a woman at the desk and watched her frown down at her computer screen and shake her head.

He went back into the archive and stood in front of the box files. Then he shrugged to himself, walked to the top-left corner of the shelving, and took down the first box.

He worked through thirty-seven boxes before he got it. I sat there, just out of view, and watched him do it. I felt sure I mustn't let him see that I was there. I was forming the idea that the map was pointing towards something those men didn't want me to find, but not because of ghosts. I crept out of the library and left the matter there. The whole thing had the sense of a foreign language about it; a language that I couldn't and perhaps didn't want to speak.

* * *

A year later I completed my dissertation. The day the results were announced I received a call from the concierge at the student residence to say I had a visitor. A man was in the hallway, an Andrew Paterson, and did I want to come down and see him? I didn't know the name and, scanning it for wordplay, couldn't detect any hint that it might be a prank by my friends. A crossed wire, I decided, or a cold caller. I said I wouldn't come down.

The concierge rang again five minutes later. 'He says it's important and he could leave a message, but he'd rather talk.'

I went downstairs, and there he was: the man from the Tradeston pub. I stopped dead in the hallway. He raised one eyebrow.

'Congratulations on the first,' he said.

I thanked him, in a prim sort of way.

'Let's go for a walk,' he said.

What did I think, then, that he wanted? Perhaps to warn me off looking any further, although the year's delay was against that. Perhaps to apologise for his theft of the notebook, though that apology would really have been owed to the library. Or perhaps to see if I knew anything else about the matter that seemed to concern him so much.

I excused myself and went back upstairs for a jacket and a sturdier pair of shoes — and a notebook and pen, just in case. I briefly considered letting someone know I'd be gone, then dismissed the idea.

He told me we could go to a pub he knew along the road. It was late in the afternoon; we might as well get a pint, he said. I followed him out of the halls and onto the road that ran along the River Kelvin, and out through quiet side streets to wherever it was he wanted to go. I wondered vaguely if I was going to be murdered.

Possibly, I thought, he knew somewhere nice and secluded where he could bash my head in. He was as big as I remembered, and as well built. He had about four decades on me, but I was certain, in that instinctive way, the silent calculations of the body, that he would have had me effortlessly in a fight.

'That's the rain coming on,' he said. This city: settling yet again into one of its glorious glooms. As we walked, squares of electric light began appearing in the high windows of the tenements — pale yellow, warm red, shrouded blue. Glasgow is a city that takes on an oppressive rain the way a drunk settles down into a drinking session. It's doing something utterly miserable that it knows exactly how to do. A great low mass of colourless cloud settles over the place like a lid, sealing it over, and the gutters swell with water, and the air smells of the rock and soil and sometimes ice of the hills. The light seeping through the cloud flexes like a subtle kind of lightning, so that the wet greys of the place seem to glow, and all available colours, whether wildflower or painted fence, have an electricity to them.

The pub was on a street at the end of a small housing estate. Paterson walked straight through to a room at the back. There was no one else there. He left me sitting at a table in the far corner, set apart from the other tables and next to a fireplace that had coal in it but no light. The carpet was truly incredible — not dissimilar, I felt, to the one in the Mitchell Library.

He returned with two pints. He settled his body down across from me. He regarded me, the nervous young man perched on the seat opposite.

'So, what's next?' he said. 'You staying on or getting a job?'

'Staying on,' I said.

Neither of us said anything for a while.

'Have you got family up here?'

'No, no. They're all down in England. In Leicester.'

There was another silence. I asked him how he'd found out who I was.

'The student newspaper,' he said. 'The folklore society photos. Great hat, by the way.'

'Ah,' I said. There'd been a quiz for the end of the year. I knew the photographs he meant. And the hat. He'd just searched for me patiently, the way he'd worked methodically through the boxes in the archive for the notebook.

He was smiling.

'You stole the notebook,' I said. 'In the archives.'

His smile faded. He watched me. 'I did,' he said.

'Well,' I said.

'What else have you got on it?'

'Nothing,' I said.

'But you're still looking into it. Folklore. That kind of thing.'

'In other areas. Nothing to do with Tradeston.'

'But you're still interested. You went out of your way to go over there.'

'Look,' I said. 'Only if — only if it's really about that sort of thing? I'm only interested in ghosts. Not in anybody's business.'

He smiled at that. 'I see.'

I found myself telling him about my dissertation. I was trying to prove to him that my interests were silly and obscure, but quickly discovered that he was prepared to listen seriously to me. I told him about my research into the Clyde and the naming of the towns and streets around it, and how I'd gone about the various pieces of work involved. Talking to him felt like talking into a recording device. You felt sure each word, each gesture, each hesitation, each cough was attended to. I'd seen this before in men that worked the land and sea. Farmers and fishermen. I hadn't seen it in Glasgow before. The city tended to produce a livelier man, fixed on his quarry like a terrier. But Paterson's attention was broad and patient.

'Bookwork,' he said when I'd finished talking. I couldn't tell if he meant this as a compliment or an insult. I sipped my pint.

'Wasn't bookwork took you down to Tradeston,' he said.

'No,' I said. 'It just – look, is it drugs or something? I won't go back, I promise. You don't need to warn me. It was just a silly thing and I don't even have the map anymore.'

'No, it's not drugs. What do you think I am?'

I could see I had offended him. I apologised.

'Okay,' he said.

'It just felt like a strange place. And then – the map, the entry in the notebook?'

He nodded.

'I just – I think it's a strange place sometimes,' I said. It was really a private thing, my obsession with weird stories, eerie fragments. But I tried to tell him about it. It felt odd to speak about it, but not so odd, with him. The way he listened.

'I don't have anything else about Tradeston,' I said. 'If that's what you wanted.'

He closed his eyes briefly in acknowledgement. He looked suddenly very alone. I wouldn't dare, even now, to say he looked vulnerable. But alone. An ageing man who'd sought out a young stranger who'd – what? Glimpsed something, or nothing, and shown up in his part of the world.

'It was mystery,' I said. 'I think I thought I'd find – it. The mystery. There's just something – and then the notebook. It's silly, that's all.'

'It's not silly,' he said. He managed to smile. 'But the thing is – maybe you're still young enough to think it's always a good idea to get to the mystery.'

'I am not,' I said. 'I'm twenty-two next month.'

We sat in silence for a while.

'I know what the map points to,' he said. 'And I've witnessed other versions of the story in that book.'

I can't begin to describe how it felt to hear him say that. He said he'd tell me what he knew. But if he was going to tell me, he'd need a promise that I wouldn't look any further for what was there. I had to put it to rest. And he wanted me to consider destroying any other indication of it that I might come across. It hadn't occurred to him, until he saw my papers that night in Tradeston, that there might be documents in archives about something like that; he was glad our paths had crossed.

'And if there are any more,' he said. 'In other places in the world, if you ever study in any other places. I don't know. If you get the feeling it's the same thing, you should leave it alone.'

He had the measure of me. I'd do as he asked, if only he'd tell me what he knew.

* * *

Paterson was sixty-three the year we spent that afternoon in the pub. He'd spent his entire working life in the construction industry — first as a labourer, then as a foreman, then as a site manager, his progression due to the loyalty he'd given one man: a Glaswegian businessman called Stuart Macrae. Paterson had spent thirty-five years under Macrae, working at all his sites across the west of Scotland.

Macrae had, from the beginning, been admired rather than liked. But Paterson knew how to work with him.

In the pub that afternoon, I watched Paterson think about how to put it into words.

'I'm not an ambitious man,' he said. 'I do a day's work and I go home. I've had my marriage and my kids. I've had all that and it's been enough. More than enough. I'm not like Macrae — it was easy for me to make room for him. Men like him wake up thinking about profit and go to sleep dreaming about profit and put themselves out there in the world to make as much of it as possible. It's not for the likes of me. But if men like him have decent conditions on a job, then men like me stick around.

'Macrae was the kind you knew would make his mark and his money. He was only thirty-five when he got the deal for the Tradeston land, and I was a young foreman at that stage. It was bad land that hadn't sold. I know it seems quaint now, that there would be a rumour like that, but that's how it was back then. But I don't think anyone actually knew about... what was there. I think people sensed something of what you sensed. It's an instinct. When they came to look at the place, they didn't put their money down. But Macrae had acumen, not instinct. He bought the Tradeston plot as part of a portfolio, as a side project. He was all through the west of Scotland already by then and was speaking about looking for investments further north. There was talk about overseas stuff and new teams being brought in — I remember it well because it unsettled me, in case it somehow put me out of work.

'He put me on as foreman for the Tradeston ground clearance. It had been sitting derelict for decades. God knows what was in it. Old machinery. Old foundations from the demolished tenements. The usual cans and knives and all that. Dirty work and heavy work — but this is what I mean about his conditions: he was paying the boys well for it. So we were a good team and it had gone as well as you could hope. But I remember going down that Friday morning relieved we'd be finished up by the afternoon. Plan was to send the boys off as soon as it was done and do the last bits of tidying myself. It had been a strange job. Nobody had come to harm, exactly. It wasn't one of the unlucky ones. It was just — there was a sick feeling about the place. A tight feeling. It put you off your food. I knew fine well the boys were working fast because they wanted off.

'We were clearing the last patch, and it was an odd thing we came across: something like old tree roots, bone-white tree roots, all tangled up in the dirt. I've not seen anything like it before or since. It all crumbled into rubble as we moved it, until we hit up against the stone.'

The stone was a cylinder about ten feet across and about six feet high. It was a pale speckled grey, and the surface had a bubbled texture to it, like a kind of fossilised leather. There was no mortar to drive the drill into; it was its own solid structure. More strangely, chisels only glanced off the surface.

'When you touched it, you didn't want to touch it for long,' Paterson said. 'There was a kind of vibration going through it. Just very slight, but enough to put your teeth on edge. So none of us wanted to climb up on it to see if there was open work at the top so we could use the drill and the excavator to pull it apart.'

Then one man said he'd a feeling it was part of a bigger structure — the stump of some enormous underground thing, not something they could just break apart.

Work came to a halt. Foreboding settled in.

The men were all working men for generations. They were men who knew fear about being maimed or electrocuted, about being poisoned by chemicals or made sick by industrial waste. There were decades of that knowledge standing in them, earned in shipyards and warehouses and on factory floors. This weird stone would surely fracture into some yawning mineshaft under their feet or turn out to be coated in some skin-melting chemical or do some other hellish thing you couldn't pay them enough to interfere with.

Paterson knew it wasn't worth fighting. And if he was being honest with himself, he felt the same. He knew he'd have to call Macrae and tell him the job had stalled. They'd maybe need specialists out, even just for a ground survey so the men would touch it again. Paterson told them they could go home. The job would have to finish on Monday instead.

One of the men, Willie Cameron, hung back and asked Paterson if he'd give him a lift home. Paterson said yes and told Cameron to wait outside while he spoke to Macrae on the phone from the work cabin.

So Cameron was outside while Paterson made the call. He was in the usual hi-vis gear. A fit, energetic type in his early thirties. Played five-a-side with some of the other men most weekends. A good worker when you got him to stop talking. Cameron was standing by the stone, nudging it with one steel-toe-capped boot then hopping backwards, as though daring himself to tolerate the vibration of it through his foot. Paterson was watching him through the window, standing in the cabin waiting for Macrae to pick up his call.

Macrae picked up and barked impatiently at Paterson, who began to explain they'd found a stone, and they couldn't move it.

Macrae wasn't getting it.

'He could be like that sometimes — he'd just decide whatever you were saying wasn't actually a problem,' Paterson said. 'It was to get you to go away and fix it without bothering him.'

But Paterson needed Macrae to agree to the specialists, so he was in the middle of explaining it again when he saw that Cameron had climbed onto the stone. He'd pulled himself onto the top of the cylinder, six feet off the ground.

'He was that kind of man — you and I would probably pull a muscle trying to climb up onto it, but he was that springy type, you know. He just got bored and went up.'

The sky was colourless. In the late afternoon the city was already growing dark. Paterson saw Cameron against the sky, standing. He saw him step towards the centre of the disc of stone; he saw him fall abruptly onto his face — suddenly heavy, as though he'd passed out. And then he saw another Cameron stand up out of Cameron's body on the stone. And that other Cameron leapt down onto the ground.

'He was on the stone and he'd jumped down as well. There were two of him. I didn't see its face, the one that jumped. And I didn't want to. If it had come towards the cabin, I don't know what I'd have done. But it went off into the waste ground. It didn't move right. It was like it had broken all its bones in the jump. And it jittered away across the ground until I lost sight of it.'

On the phone, Macrae shouted at Paterson to speak.

'Stuart,' Paterson whispered, 'I need you to come down here.'

Macrae was furious. He didn't think Paterson was making sense. But something in the tone of Paterson's voice made him do as he asked.

'I phoned the ambulance,' Paterson said. 'I couldn't see how to get him off the thing myself and — nothing would have made me touch him.'

The paramedics arrived at the same time as Macrae's Rover swung onto the waste land. Paterson told the paramedics he thought the stone might be poisonous, that they shouldn't go up. They listened to him and worked from the ground to lift Cameron down onto a stretcher. Cameron was still breathing. The paramedics said they were taking him to the Royal. Then Paterson and Macrae were left standing on the waste ground. A light rain was falling. The sky was a heavier grey.

'Macrae asked me what the fuck had gone wrong,' Paterson said. 'We went into the cabin. I needed whisky but the only thing we had was tea. I was already starting to doubt myself. I mean — how could it have been? How could I have seen that? I knew I had, but —'

Paterson sighed. 'This is probably more than you need, but I'll tell you what it was like. It was like when I was a wee boy — far too wee to see something like that — and I saw my father hit my mother. They were in their bedroom, and they didn't know I'd come up the stairs and onto the landing. It was the same feeling. Mum and dad loved each other. I'd seen it, but I couldn't have seen it. I had the sound and the pictures, but I couldn't have the sense of it.'

It was this feeling — that he'd met this seeing and not seeing before, that gave Paterson the courage to tell Macrae what he'd seen.

'He just stared at me. Then he started to laugh. I never could abide that in him — it's not even a laugh, it's just a mocking sound. It's the sound people make when they want you to know how little they think of you.

'Macrae said I'd better get the specialists down to look at it then, and maybe a psychiatrist while I was at it. It was the only time I refused an order from him. I told him if he wanted any more work on that place, he could find another man or he could do it himself.

'I think he thought I was coming over all macho or something, but I was afraid. I was feart. And I was stuck there in the cabin with him because I was too afraid to go out in case it came back. And what if the thing out there was Cameron, and we'd sent the wrong thing to the hospital, and he was out there somewhere in the rain, his bones all broken?

'Macrae just shrugged his shoulders at me. Said he wasn't wasting any more of his time. I followed him out onto the waste ground. He got into his Rover and I got into my van.'

Paterson didn't hear from Macrae over the weekend. He started to think maybe he didn't have a job anymore. But early on Monday morning his phone rang at home.

'It was Macrae. But his voice was strange. Hollow sounding. Then he said Willie Cameron had died. I thought he'd just called to tell me that, but he stayed on the line. Said he wanted me back down at the site as soon as I was able. I was maybe going to tell him no. I'd been thinking — there were other places that would take me. I'd been too comfortable with Macrae and it was just laziness not to move on after he spoke to me like that. And I'd had plenty of time over the weekend to doubt myself again — I'd made an embarrassment of myself with him and didn't really want to see him.

'But he was a businessman, remember. He knew when he wasn't about to close a deal. He said he'd give me a raise — half my wages again on top — to stay on with him. I thought I'd misheard him. But he said he'd realised it was time he recognised the good men he had and if I wanted it the offer was there. I thought the death of Willie must have got to him. He'd gone sentimental. I asked him if he'd heard anything about what happened to Willie, whether he'd heard anything from the doctors. There was a big silence. I know now what he wasn't saying, but I didn't then.

'"I went up to see him," Macrae said. He stopped speaking and coughed. "Heart failure. Just bad luck, they think. He climbed up on that stone and it caught up with him — it happens, apparently. People can have these problems and never know until it kills them." He started coughing again. It was a dry rattle.

'"It's terrible," I said.

'"It is, Andy," he said, and he never used my first name. That was as close as he'd get to pleading with me. I knew that.

"'I'll take that raise, if you're offering," I said. I remember there was a pause. And when he started speaking again there was a catch in his voice.

"'Good man," he said. "Good man."

'I went down to the site to meet him. When I drove into the site, I saw a metal shed standing over the spot where the stone had been. Just one of those DIY prefab ones you can put up in an hour or two. He must have done it himself. The door was padlocked, although that wouldn't have stopped anybody with a crowbar. Macrae saw me looking at it.

'It's not moveable without deep drilling,' he said. 'The stone. I want a dummy unit built round it. So we don't have anybody interfering with it. I want nobody inside that shed, do you hear me? Not even you.'

'That was him back to his normal self, I thought. You'd think I was raring to get into his rubbish wee shed. "Not a problem," I said.

'He had the plans for the unit and said he'd supervise with me, and it would need six more bodies. It took four days, working stupid hours, and he was there for the whole thing. He was the first on site and last to leave. He didn't look well. Pale, and kind of stiff seeming, the way he moved. I told him to get a rest at one point and he acted like he hadn't heard me. It was odd having him on site. Still in the fancy business suit but working like a foreman.

'We built a standard industrial estate unit, with a reception in front so that from the outside it would look the same as the others we'd build fully. But inside this one there was only the shed. There were no utilities running to it. Macrae planned for it never to be used.

'There were only four boys on the job on the last day, and they were doing the finishing touches outside. All four of them were up working on the guttering and the roof when Macrae said he'd go and get the morning rolls from the van. I said I'd do it. The thought of Macrae himself going to the roll van — I mean, if you'd met wee Sandra, and the thought of him — '

Paterson stopped and smiled at me. 'You know what I mean. Anyway, off he went. It was only round the corner, so he walked. And he'd left his keys in his Rover, and when I tried the driver's door it wasn't locked. I knew Macrae would be a while at the van. And I knew the lads would be a while on the roof. So I took the keys and went into the unit. He'd been so secretive about it, and I'd half a mind he'd had some sort of government specialist down and it would be all marked up with hazard tape. I think I wanted to see some sort of proof of that — evidence of how dangerous it was, even if no one was going to believe me about Willie.

'I had a wee pen torch on my belt that was enough to see by. There was already dust settling, and there was the shed in the middle. There was a strange feeling — like the way you feel the ground rumbling when you're above the subway line at Tollcross. And my face felt tight as well.'

Here, Paterson indicated his sinuses.

'I tried the keys on the padlock for the shed. When one slid into place I just stood there. It took me a minute to turn it and unlock it. I unhooked it and opened the door just enough to peer in with the torch. I didn't go in.

'There was no hazard tape or official notice or anything like that. Macrae had just put a white sheet over the top of it. Just the usual sheeting we'd use for a painting job. It was draped over the top of the cylinder. Or maybe it was draped over something on top of the cylinder. I couldn't see much — just — the sheet looked lumpy and bunched up over something large, about the size of a man, lying on top of the stone. But — I just didn't let myself see it. I couldn't bring myself to go any closer or even think about lifting the sheet. I just swept the beam of the torch away and pushed the shed door shut and locked it. I got myself out of there and put the keys back into Macrae's car.

'The dummy unit was locked up later that day. And, not long after that, the rest of the units were built. Although investors had been shy about buying the land, plenty of businesses were happy to fill the premises: the usual mix of tradesmen, offices, wholesalers turned up. All Macrae asked me to do was keep an eye on the site maintenance, and that's no job really, it was no problem at all. He had me working on other projects and sites – and he kept my pay at the new high rate and there was never a further word about it. Every year he added a raise, and a decent one as well.

'I felt lucky with it all. I liked the work well enough and the pay was great. After that one moment the night of the stone, the way he'd spoken to me, I never had a bad word off him. We worked well together – I knew how to deal with him and I did as I was told.

'So I stuck with him. And the thing was: he never moved. There had always been the expectation with Macrae that there would be overseas investments, that he'd branch out, all that. But he never did. He stayed west of Scotland. He seemed to have reached a point, after the Tradeston development, that he never quite surpassed. He did well – he was a rich man, by any sensible standard – but if you knew him at all you knew he'd stalled.

'But that suited me. I got more responsibility – he seemed to have taken to trusting me. Thing was, he never looked well. And after a while he had this air about him. He was like a lost wee boy when it was just the two of us. Like he could put on a show for the boardroom types. The kind of men that always made me feel like my boots were too dirty. But when it was just us two, all that fell away, and he was lost. He seemed to be looking to me for something.

'It maybe embarrassed me a bit. I didn't know what to do with it. But after a while I worked out he just wanted me to be who I was. Not a businessman like him. Just solid, competent, consistent. He got this look of relief when we worked something out together about a site or an installation.

'He sometimes asked me if I was still happy working for him. Every year or so that would come up, like it built up in him as a constant worry until he had to say something again.

'I did wonder what was going on with him. But it wasn't — he was hardly what you or I or most people would think of as a failure. It was up to him how he wanted to conduct himself.

'He was odd when I settled down with Mary. He did all the right things — the gift, the card, the things you're meant to say. But when I invited him to the wedding, he said right away that he couldn't make it. Then he was strange with me for a while. Distant. I maybe wondered if he played the other way then, but that wasn't any of my business either.

'But there was a woman on the scene shortly afterwards. She didn't last long — I mean, maybe months. Then there was another, and it was the same with her. I didn't see him with anyone after that. He'd have been in his early forties by then.

'When Mary and I had our first wee girl he did it all again: the gift, the card, the right words. But all totally off somehow. By then I think I knew he had some sort of health problem. He'd a terrible colour to him. Macrae was an athletic type, not bulky like me. Tidy, sporty looking. Posture like a soldier. And he still had all that, even as his hair turned grey, but he'd gone waxy looking as well, like the blood wasn't reaching the skin. Like you could break off a piece of him like soft clay. We'd be in his office, just him and me, and it was like I'd suddenly see how he really looked, and I'd need to breathe and calm myself down, stop myself from running screaming out the room.

'There are all sorts of disorders you get — blood things, or — somebody said maybe an immune thing. But over the years people saw less of him anyway. He gave a lot of the work over to me. And my wages kept going up, and we had good conditions for the workers, and if Macrae's businesses never went beyond a certain point, they were still doing well. And among all that I had another wee girl, and then both my wee girls grew up and we sent them off to university.'

Paterson stopped there for a moment.

'After the girls were both away studying,' he said, 'Mary took ill. Cancer. It was — it was really fucking awful. Macrae was good about it. Said as long as I got the work done I was to make sure I got to her appointments and whatever else she needed. And if I couldn't get the work done just to let him know. Mary was more worried about the girls and their exams than herself. But Macrae was — I think a different fear had settled on him by then. He knew he had my loyalty; now it was about whether or not I was keeping well myself. The last thing he needed was for me not to cope with what was happening to Mary. In the end I took a month off — I'd two weeks at the end with her. And the rest of the time was the funeral and all that. And then I just worked after that. Saw the girls as often as I could.'

'I'm sorry,' I said to Paterson.

He smiled at me. 'So am I, son. So am I.'

By this time, Paterson explained, he was about to turn fifty, and Macrae had just turned sixty. They entered the 1990s, and the world around them changed rapidly: faster, busier, more global, more technological. But Tradeston, and Macrae's small part of it, continued as it always had. Factories and showrooms lay empty; the sun rose and fell; cracks in the windows appeared, and entire buildings slid into dust. Heavier industry moved in — welding and fabrication and God knows what else.

'He received an offer to sell the estate,' Paterson said. 'He told me he'd refuse it. But he was past retirement age by then. I told him I didn't think he needed to be turning up every day and sitting in the back office — I thought he should think about selling it off and looking after himself. It was time to bring things to an end, I said. He was very thin, but not frail. You've never seen anything like it. He'd thinned away like a rock in bad weather, not like a man who was sick and getting old. He still had that upright posture, even though he had this odd, broken-boned way of moving when he walked.

'I used to have nightmares about it. They started after Mary died. I'd dream I was sitting in our garden, but the tall fences were gone, and there was a broad sunny meadow there instead, and I'd see a figure in the distance coming towards me. Always, at first, I'd think it must be Mary. And then I'd recognise the walk and know it was him.

'Macrae said he'd think about what I said. He said — and I'll never forget this — "That's your advice, is it? To bring things to an end?"

'And I said: "Yes, it is."

'I got a phone call later that night from him. It was a Friday — I thought he must've fallen ill and needed help. But he sounded the same as he always did. And he was asking me to go down to the estate and meet him. The following night. Saturday, at half past ten.

'The place was dead. There were a few cars at the perimeter of the estate — the new money, the drugs. But down at Macrae's it was quiet. He'd switched the lights on at his office and I parked the car and went in. He was sitting at his desk. And he'd a bottle of whisky and two tumblers sitting out. He asked me to take a seat and offered me a drink. When he placed the glass in front of me, his hand was waxy and the fingernails were grey.

'"So what's all this about," I said. I was trying to keep the tone light. He told me he'd thought about things and that I was right.

'"Good," I said. "That's good, Stuart."

'He looked at me when I used his first name — he was always Macrae to me, even after thirty years. Just for a moment there was a glimpse of the man I'd known, back when he'd bought the place and Cameron had died. Thirty-five years old. As if it was only me who'd done the past thirty years of living.

'"You've been good to me," Macrae said. I supposed I had. I'd put the work in for him.

'"You've been good to me as well," I said. I realised he'd intended the meeting and the whisky as a kind of celebration. And this was his idea of it: the site office, late on a Saturday, just the two of us. It was a sad, painful kind of thing. I almost couldn't bear it.

'You never saw him smile, but he managed to smile at me then. And it was a terrible thing, on his face, and I understood why he didn't do it.

'He watched me take a sip of the whisky. "I should have listened to you," he said.

'"I thought you just did," I said.

'"Not about the sale," he said. He couldn't seem to speak for a long time. Then he sighed and rubbed one of his pale wax hands over his eyes.

'"Do you know I wish I could cry?" he said. "It's a terrible thing, not to be able to cry."

'"Stuart, maybe you need to talk to someone," I said. He was frightening me. I was sorry for him, but I also didn't feel sure of him. He drained his whisky. He set the glass down slowly, like he knew I was getting afraid and didn't want to make it worse. That helped; it did calm me down a bit.

'"I mean I should've listened to you when Willie Cameron died," he said.

'I watched him. He'd shocked me, bringing that name up.

"'All that's a long time ago," I said.

"'I went up to the Royal to see him," Macrae said. "It wasn't visiting hours but — you know what I'm like. What I was like. I sweet-talked the nurse and she let me in. It was late. He was in one of the wards that look out over the graveyard. So there were the headstones and the steep wall of the hill outside. It was all dark at that time of night, except for a few lights down towards the street level and the cathedral.

"'He was in a coma. I'd said I was worried for him and just wanted to pay my respects — just in case he didn't last the night. And that was true. But I also wanted to see how bad it looked. I was worried there would be some sort of case against me, some sort of thing the family could pin on the company." Macrae sighed. "Anyway, the thing was — he died while I was in the room. All sorts of alarms went off and all sorts of people rushed in, and I stood right back by the windows. And I saw him. He was coming down the hill at the Necropolis into the street. In his orange hi-vis from the site. He was dying in the bed and the other half of him was coming down towards the hospital. Outside, coming down the hill; inside, dying on the bed. I saw it. And you'd told me."

'I didn't know what to say to him. I thought of the sleepless nights afterwards, the way I'd felt, quietly, in one corner of my mind, that maybe I'd made it all up, maybe I was going mad. I'd put it away eventually, but it had worried me for a long time. And the worry was still in me, because when Macrae said what he said, I felt it change. It was like a knot loosening. It had held tight in me all this time.

"'I wish you'd told me sooner," I said.

"'I know," he said.

"'But it's all over now anyway," I said, although even as I said it, I knew that wasn't true. Macrae made that sad, terrible smile again. All this time, I'd known. But I hadn't let myself know.

'"After I left the hospital," Macrae said, "I came back here. I just wanted to look at the thing. I think I was angry with you. I was angry that you were right after how I'd spoken to you. I'd thought you were talking such total nonsense and then — I just wanted to see it for myself. And I did. I climbed up onto it and I looked down."

'He was quiet for a long time. The clock in the site office ticked. The sickly electric light shone through the whisky glasses and over his pale skin.

'"I saw," he said. "My God, I saw."

'The thing was: I saw him wince when he said the Lord's name. It's the first time I understood — really felt it, in my body — why the Catholics cross themselves. I felt the need to be able to make some sign to protect myself. I'll never forget it. Sitting there, with my hands on my knees, feeling that they were empty, and there was nothing I could do.

'He straightened some papers on his desk. "I think," he said, "if I lift it down, I'll walk into it. And die, like Willie did. At least I fucking hope so." He gave a dry, hopeless laugh. He forced himself to lift his eyes from the papers on his desk. "Best get it sorted now."

'I knew what he was saying, but I couldn't seem to speak. He told me he'd lived, after a fashion, for the past thirty years. He said he rarely slept and could not love. He'd worked and worked and waited for his body to die. But he knew now it would go on and on unless he dragged himself off the stone. He had to end it. It was up to him.

'"But if you could be there, Andy," he said. "If you could help. And I need things to be right for you afterwards — the story is you found me, and you phoned an ambulance. You suppose I must have crawled off into one of the empty units after starting the drinking too early. I hadn't been well for a long time. You're not surprised it all became too much. I suppose it'll be heart failure, like Willie Cameron. And you'll get me a funeral with a minister to say a few words. Please. Because I think — I'll need it. And I haven't been able to go to — it hasn't let me go to them. And then you'll have concrete poured all over it and have it sealed off at that level across the whole site. The concrete will fill the eye of it — I think even if the level of concrete is cleared, they'd still need to get the concrete out of the eye before it could work itself again. Please, Andy. I'm asking you. I'm not ordering."

'"Of course I'll do it," I said. I told him I was sorry for him, and he said again that he wished he could cry.

'He'd thought it all through like he did with any business deal. He'd let the CCTV tape run empty on the Friday night. So there had been nothing to record me arriving at the site on Saturday, and there was nothing to record the two of us walking across the tarmac from the site office to the dummy unit. The unit still had dummy signage in the windows, although faded now and dated looking, and the windows had been kept clean on the outside. But inside the dust was thick on the floor. We made our way over to the shed by torchlight. It was just as we'd left it.

'Macrae limped over and stood there. I waited a good few steps behind him. I knew he was working up the nerve to open it. Eventually, he reached out and undid the padlock. Then he waited for me. I walked up and went inside with him and could see the stone was still there, still covered in the white sheet. Underneath the sheet was the outline of a leg, a foot, a body. Macrae dragged the sheet down. And there he was, lying face down on the stone. And he was standing next to me with the sheet in his hands.

'On the stone his eyes were closed. His body was splayed out across the top, just like the way Willie Cameron had fallen. The body on the stone looked the way Macrae had looked all those years ago, except desiccated, fragile somehow. But not dead.

'I didn't know if I could make myself touch it. But I wanted to do it for him. It's not that I felt I owed him it; I just wanted to do right by him. I kept my head down and followed his orders. He told me to lift at the legs and he would take the arms.

'The legs felt papery in my hands, under the cloth of the trousers. There wasn't much weight to it. We got it down and we carried him out of the shed, into the main space of the unit. We laid him down on the floor.

'"I'm sorry, Stuart," I said. He looked at me but didn't speak. I believe he heard me; I'm glad I was there with him. Something slid in his face — it went out of joint, the same way his limbs already didn't quite fit. He fell to his crooked knees. He was like that for a moment then he fell forwards and crawled over himself, that juddering way, like the way Cameron had moved. He merged into his body. I saw it. I watched him do it. And the body was different, more human again once he'd done it. It filled out. But it didn't move.

'I did everything like he said: I covered the stone with the sheet and locked the shed with the padlock. Then I went to the site office and called for an ambulance. He was dead and they took him away. The police called me, and I gave them the story Macrae had told me to give them. I arranged a funeral and a minister just as he'd asked. I made absolutely sure he had that.

'I got the concrete poured into it — I did it blindly from the ground. I did it myself so no one else would run the risk of looking down into that thing. And I started setting up the arrangements to concrete that whole part of the site.

'A few weeks later I received a call from a lawyer, to let me know about the money Macrae had left for my daughters. And that was it. That was that.'

* * *

Paterson sighed. The pub was cosy and quiet around us. The Glasgow rain ran merrily down the windows, and the murmur of men's voices reached us from the bar. I realised I'd thought of the city as a game I was playing, but it didn't feel like that now. Paterson sat across from me peacefully. He was a big man who had all his city singing through him. He never did tell me exactly where the stone had been, and by then I knew better than to ask.

Lauren O'Donoghue's first Fiction Desk story is an evocative exploration of the spaces that open up between our inner lives and our friendships.

Black Hill
Lauren O'Donoghue

In summer the view from Black Hill is almost laughably perfect; a nationalist's wet dream of an English pastoral, a tableau to be shot in soft-focus and set to a choirboy rendition of Jerusalem. That's how Rachel remembers this place, when she's back in Manchester; the way she describes it, lovingly, to her city-born friends.

It isn't summer today, though. It's the grimmest, dirtiest point in December, and the mizzling rain has obscured the view altogether. It makes the peak of the hill feel oddly claustrophobic. An island in a sea of fog, covered in wet grass and rabbit shit. Caspar Friedrich with low-grade depression.

Rachel has only seen one other pair of hikers since she met Megan in the car park. They were out-of-towners. She could tell from the ambitious poles they carried, the fluorescent tabards worn over Peter Storm anoraks. Rachel once saw a whole troupe of these types, similarly outfitted and roped together at the waist, fall down the slope of Black Hill. One tripped on a loose patch of scree and slipped, sending the others toppling — comically slowly — like dominoes in crampons and gilets.

Rachel and Megan are not dressed for a hike. They are locals, though neither of them has lived here in fifteen years, and locals do not bother with the gear. Megan is wearing a parka and Converse. Rachel has on a denim jacket and ankle boots. Rachel feels, as she always does when she returns to their hometown, superior to the well-equipped weekenders. Her mastery of the landscape supersedes the need for specialist clothing.

She also feels damp, and thoroughly miserable. The thin rain sticks her jeans to her thighs, which are cold and puckered as a raw chicken, and creeps down the collar of her sweatshirt.

Megan has been talking about her recent break-up for forty-five minutes.

'I think the worst part of it,' Megan says, 'is the lost time. It's like — you start thinking about the future, don't you? It's not like before when you could just, I don't know, build a relationship around a mutual love of M83 and pills. Our *lifestyles* were compatible.'

'Yeah,' Rachel says. 'I get you.'

'It's my fault —'

'No it's not,' Rachel says, automatically. 'He's the one who —'

'No, Rach, let me finish.' Megan wipes some of the damp from her cheeks with the cuff of her parka. She does this with great dignity, imbuing the gesture with an almost saintly poise. Megan is one of those women who has turned being wounded into a fine art. 'It *is* my fault, because I didn't ask him. I just assumed I knew what he wanted. I mean, not everyone wants to settle down, do they?'

'No,' Rachel says, ignoring the possible jibe, 'but —'

'If I'd just asked him if he wanted something serious, this wouldn't have happened. I'm the one who made assumptions.'

In Rachel's private opinion, if you're a thirty-four-year-old man with no intention of settling down, the onus is probably on you to mention that when you enter a relationship. She knows better than to say this, however. Megan is still in the raw, defensive phase of her breakup. She will brook no insult towards Tony, irrespective of the fact that he has just ended their relationship — by text! — five days before Christmas.

'Communication is a two-way street,' Rachel says, falling back into the safety of platitudes. 'He should have been honest with you at the start.'

'Maybe.' Megan sniffs prettily, then loops her arm through the crook of Rachel's elbow. It's a familiar gesture. They used to walk like this in school, heads ducked low and close together while they discussed the week's gossip; who was texting Sarah's older brother, who had been excluded for smoking in the science block toilets, who got fingered in the bushes behind the bowling green.

The casual intimacy gives Rachel a rare pang of nostalgia. She feels no particular yearning for her teenage years, but there's something about coming home for Christmas that makes her ripe for sentimentality. It's the urge to revert to a time when every detail of her life was deeply important to someone else; when the act of buying eyeshadow or changing her status on MSN Messenger was one of the utmost gravity.

She slides her hand down to Megan's wrist and grips it tightly, using her for leverage as she steps onto the jagged rocks near the summit. These granite shelves that jut from the hillside are treacherous today, made smooth and slippery with rain. In the middle distance Rachel can make out a dim, three-pronged shape, like a giant raising its arms towards the sky. The tree's silhouette reorients her, provides a landmark to navigate around.

'Six months is a longer time than you think,' Megan says, unprompted. 'It doesn't sound like much, but God — think of what I could have been doing. It's hard, feeling like you've lost those months, you know?'

Rachel almost tells her then. *Yes, Megan, I know. I've been seeing someone for the past two years and that's not going anywhere either.* A dark little thrill runs down her spine at the thought. She's considered disclosing her relationship to Megan and the others numerous times, but has always thought better of it. There are four reasons for this, all to do with the person with whom Rachel is sleeping — her boss (1), a fifty-something (2) married (3) woman (4).

If Rachel were to share this information with her hometown friends, it would only be for the initial, fleeting pleasure of scandalising them. The same triumph she'd once felt announcing that she'd tried coke at a party, or pulling down her jeans to reveal the butterfly tattooed on her hip; satisfying, but ephemeral. Their initial shock would swiftly fade to concern, then confusion, finally settling on discomfort. Then someone would change the subject, and it would never be spoken of again.

Rachel made a half-hearted attempt to come out to them once. They have a group chat — 'st pauls back row gals' — where they semi-regularly share details of their lives and reminisce abouts incidents from their school days. About four years ago Rachel met a woman called Maria on a dating app, and the two of them had arranged to get a drink together. Seeing an opportunity, she had messaged the group chat *date tomorrow! what to wear?*

This elicited all of the predictable *ooh! eek!* exclamations, and then, as Rachel had hoped, someone asked *what's he like?*

not he, she had replied, blood pounding uncomfortably in her ears. *she*

It took a full five minutes for the first response to come. *oh cool :)* it said. *jeans and a nice top maybe?*

The conversation had continued like this, awkward and truncated, until Helen asked for advice about a job interview and everyone started talking about that instead. Rachel couldn't blame them. It wasn't that they were homophobic — far from it — it was simply that they couldn't see themselves reflected in Rachel's experience, couldn't picture themselves in her position. They were all so profoundly, neatly heterosexual that the concept of queer desire didn't register properly in their brains. Imagining a scenario where they could be attracted to a woman caused them to freeze, like a laptop with too many tabs open.

Rachel sympathises with this. It is the same alienation that prevents her from understanding when her friends have their hearts broken by men named Ian, who wear Wrangler jeans and drive low-end Audis. Rachel is attracted to men sometimes, but largely in an abstract, theoretical way, and has never managed to form an attachment to one. Women love each other viciously, with claws and teeth. Most men, as far as Rachel can tell, occupy an emotional space somewhere between indifferent and withholding. Producing soap opera levels of distress over the loss of one is incomprehensible to her.

She came to accept this gulf of understanding a long time ago. It is no great loss, not being able to share the details of her love life with her school friends. Very few of the people in her life these days are straight, and there are plenty who know about Natasha. She isn't desperate for a confidante or in need of advice. Still — in this moment she wishes she could talk to Megan, at least. The two of them were closer than the others, when they were teenagers. It was Megan who had given Rachel her first piercing, with a blunt stud and a slice of apple, lying on Megan's bedroom floor half-cut on her mum's cherry brandy. Rachel was the one who covered for Megan when she got the sleeper train up to Glasgow, to spend the weekend with a boy she'd met on a MySpace forum.

Now Megan is seeking that same camaraderie, wanting Rachel to be there for her in her time of need, and Rachel can't provide it because she'll never be able to reciprocate. She can make all the right noises, yes, give the same advice you'd get in any Agony Aunt column, but she can't invest in Megan's pain. Not really. Because all the time Rachel is thinking about how she's not saying *my girlfriend's at home with her husband and kids right now, and it's making me want to shove my fingers down my throat.* And how she wants to say *grow up and get over it, he was a prick anyway, he used Lynx Africa body wash and thought Michael McIntyre was funny.* It's an ugly urge, this desire towards cruelty, one she hates feeling in herself.

Last week, just before she travelled home, Rachel had gone to see Natasha at her house in Chorlton. Natasha's husband — Rachel knows his name, but hates saying it — had taken the kids to visit their cousins in Birmingham for the weekend, and Natasha had invented a migraine that prevented her from travelling with them. Rachel didn't know whether Natasha's husband had been convinced by this lie, and didn't ask. She knocked round the side door when she arrived, feeling furtive and sleazy and a little turned on, and was ushered inside before the neighbours saw.

Rachel fucked Natasha against the kitchen island, one hand down the waistband of her Boden leggings and the other tangled in her hair. She has beautiful hair — soft and thick, undyed despite the streaks of grey. Rachel likes to wrap strands of it around her fingers, leaving bird's-nest tangles behind. Little markers of her presence. Once it was over they leaned together, breathing hard, surrounded by Le Creuset skillets and Ottolenghi cookbooks and the photos of Natasha's children that stared, cherubic and accusatory, out from the fridge.

'You can't stay,' Natasha said, her breath tickling the shell of Rachel's ear. 'I don't know what time they'll be back tomorrow. I'm sorry.'

'It's okay,' Rachel said, though it wasn't. 'I'm just glad you were free tonight.'

'Me too, darling.'

Every time Natasha calls her *darling* Rachel wants to howl at the moon, to flay herself to the bone. The love she has for this woman is a natural disaster, tectonic and destructive. She has never asked Natasha to leave her husband, because she knows the answer and has no desire to hear it. The point of this affair is not to be happy ever after. The point is to dash herself against the rocks of love until there is nothing left. It is the same urge that once drove her to spark cheap Bic lighters under her arm, to hold the flame there until the skin reddened and blistered.

'When do I have to go?' Rachel asked, hating the desperation in her voice. She has maintained the relationship for this long only by concealing the depth of her feelings; every time she slips into neediness Natasha seizes up.

'Give it an hour,' Natasha said, extricating herself from Rachel's arms and smoothing down the front of her shirt. 'Andrea next door gets home late on Fridays. I'd rather she didn't see you leaving.'

Rachel chose to hear *I want to spend more time with you*. This was, it had to be said, likely not untrue. Natasha fixed them both a drink — campari and soda, garnished with a slice of blood orange — and for a while they simply talked, curled together on the sofa in front of the wood burner. A large tabby cat sat on the fire-warmed flagstones, glaring suspiciously up at Rachel. Recognising her as an interloper. Rachel didn't care, or had become so accustomed to trying that she could believe that she didn't. Borrowed domesticity was preferable to the real kind, she told herself. She didn't have to think about school runs, or clean litter trays, or have listless missionary sex with a man she'd ceased to love a decade ago. No, Rachel occupied the shallow, magazine-cover parts of Natasha's life. Drinking her cocktails, using her Molton Brown hand cream, making her come with a White Company throw between her teeth. A relationship charted in tasteful lifestyle brands.

When they reach the very top of the hill Rachel thinks again about telling Megan. She wants to confide in her the way they used to, to have the same rapt attention given to her secrets. Among all of the St. Paul's girls, Megan would be the most likely to take her seriously. But knowing this makes the prospect of her rejection all the worse. Rachel imagines the way Megan might unconsciously let go of her arm, the strained note that might enter her voice as she says *wow, Rach, really?* No. Not worth the risk.

'See that tree?' Rachel says instead, pointing at the bare shape of it looming out of the fog. 'I used to be obsessed with it when I was a kid.'

Megan snorts. 'Obsessed with a tree?'

'Yeah,' Rachel says, turning sideways to shuffle down the slope towards it. 'I was dead into fairies when I was little. Remember those books, where they had fairies for all the different flowers?'

'I think so. The geranium fairy, stuff like that?'

Rachel nods. 'We used to come on walks up here sometimes, and I was fucking *convinced* that tree had fairies living in it.'

'Oh, bless. That's proper only-child stuff.'

'Shut up.'

'It is!'

'Anyway.' Rachel grips Megan's hand as the two of them navigate carefully down the side of Black Hill. The rain has stopped now, but the ground is saturated and slippery underfoot. 'One day we came up here – must have been what, seven? – and there's a tiny bunch of flowers between the roots.' She holds her thumb and finger two inches apart. 'Like, this big.'

'What, like growing?'

'No, like someone put them there. Obviously I went nuts. Thought the fairies had left them for me.'

Megan's forehead creases, her bottom lip pushing out slightly. It's an expression of pure, unbridled affection, the kind you only share with people you've known for a long time. 'That's really cute, Rach.'

'Isn't it?' she says, turning her attention back to the placement of her feet. 'It was probably just Ledbury hippies, but you know. It was exciting at the time.'

Rachel has never told anyone about the flowers before. Even at the time she concealed it from her parents, understanding somehow that what she had found was secret, and that exposing it to other people would spoil it somehow. She offers it to Megan now as a consolation of sorts; a secret in exchange for the one that stays unspoken.

Megan chooses that moment to step into the mouth of a rabbit hole, twisting her ankle sideways and almost pulling Rachel down with her. They somehow manage to remain upright, windmilling their arms and planting their feet against the slick earth, shrieking with laughter once the danger has passed. They cling to each other, cackling, and for a second Rachel is fourteen again, she and Megan wobbling up the hill in their kitten heels, eyes black-rimmed and owlish, hiking to the summit on the promise of cider and cigarettes and, if they're lucky, some truly atrocious weed. She fights to catch her breath as she rights herself, craning her neck to dab her eyes with the shoulder of her jacket.

'Fucking hell,' Megan says. 'Whose idea was this?'

'Yours. You said, "I'm sad, Rach, I need to walk it out."'

'Oh yeah. Shit idea.'

'Pub?'

'God, yes.'

They make it down without incident, leaving the hiking trail for the road that bisects the hill on the county line. By the time they reach the King's Arms the weather has cleared a little, the fog lifting to reveal saturated fields and a sky the colour of dirty snow. Shafts of sunlight break through the distant clouds, falling on the forested slopes of the valley like a blessing. Rachel fills her lungs with air, longing for that familiar wet-earth scent of her childhood, but smells only the cold.

The parlour of the pub is quiet, few people having ventured out that day, and Rachel and Megan manage to claim a spot by the fire. They peel themselves out of their coats, shivering, debate whether it would be appropriate to take off their shoes as well. Megan buys two pints of something hoppy and local, along with several packets of crisps. They pass a few pleasant hours this way, drinking and talking and letting the warmth leech back into their bones. When Megan talks about Tony — which she does only a little — she tones down her wronged-innocent demeanour slightly. She even manages to call him a twat.

Rachel's stomach is empty, and she is fairly drunk by her third pint. When Megan goes to buy another round Rachel excuses herself, saying that she needs to get some air.

It's on the cusp of getting dark, though it's barely three in the afternoon. The sky to the east is the colour of a fresh bruise. Rachel has left her jacket inside, and her arms prickle with gooseflesh as she gropes for her phone in the pocket of her jeans. Once she pulls it out she taps the screen with numb fingers, feels a surge of heat in her chest as she lifts it to her ear.

One ring. Two. Three. Rachel is on the verge of hanging up when there's a crackle on the line, a short clearing of a throat. She can hear music in the background, voices. A Christmas party soundscape.

'Hello?' Natasha says.

Rachel blinks hard, wets her lips with the tip of her tongue. 'Hi,' she says. 'I – I just wanted to hear your voice.'

A pause. In the background of the call a child screams, high and delighted. There's a noise like Velcro tearing, and then Natasha's voice again, muffled this time. 'I told you,' she says. 'Just one of those spam calls.' Another voice – male – answers, though the sound is little more than a grunt.

'Sorry if it's a bad time.' Rachel enunciates carefully to counteract the slurring of her words. 'Just say when I can call back. I miss you.'

'Take us off your list, please. Don't call again.'

Another crackle before, abruptly, silence. Rachel stands with the phone held against her ear for a long moment, unmoving. As though time would remain inert if she could just stay perfectly still. Like she can prevent it, somehow, from galloping off into the future, from dragging her into the inevitability of what happens next. Either the screen is very cold where it touches her skin, or her skin is very hot where it touches the screen. There is a sourness at the back of her tongue that has nothing to do with drinking.

The cloud forms of the early afternoon have flattened to a panel of grey, and a dark spot against the dim sky draws Rachel's attention. She turns to focus on it, and the details of its shape materialise; a bird, hovering almost motionless above the western slope of the hill. When it dives Rachel has the distinct impression that the world is turning sideways on its axis, the ground lurching upwards while the bird remains suspended in the air. She knows a brief, sharp moment of panic, a crushing in her chest at this sudden skewing of her vision. Then the dark form is lost among the trees, and Rachel comes back to herself; cold, breathing shallow, her phone still pressed against her ear.

In the space of a minute the world has fractured and reformed itself, and she is the only one who has witnessed it. She will have to carry it with her now, this knowledge; this understanding that things are not as they were, nor ever will be again. It is a revelation that will belong to her alone.

A sudden wind, bitter cold, whips in through the cutting. The shadow of Black Hill looms in quiet judgement. Rachel shivers, returns her phone to her pocket, and turns to walk back inside.

A trip taken with the hope of revitalising a relationship instead gives the protagonist an opportunity to catch up with herself in Ian Critchley's first Fiction Desk story.

Ghost Walks
Ian Critchley

'Welcome, welcome, come nearer, don't be shy. Call me Ishmael. Or Bob. Whatever takes your fancy. How many of us are there? One, two, three ... nine, ten, eleven, twelve. Thirteen, including me. Unlucky for some.'

Sarah rolled her eyes. The guide was tall and dressed as an undertaker, top hat and all. Despite the mizzle, his umbrella remained furled.

It was Tom who'd seen the sign earlier that afternoon, soon after they'd arrived in the city: 'Come and be terrified by ghostly tales of terror.'

'Might be fun,' he'd said.

They'd gathered at dusk by the minster's west front. Arc lights illuminated the statues and the gargoyles. Beside Sarah stood a family of four, the kids no more than five or six. A group of women

– a hen party? – giggled into canned cocktails. A couple, teenagers maybe, held hands, their eyes shining bright in the darkness. She and Tom had been like that once.

Ishmael/Bob brandished his umbrella like a sword. 'The minster. Built on the sweat and the blood of hundreds of workers. Stone by stone by stone. Tough work. Physical work. Stressful work. Two of the builders, John and Joseph, were sworn enemies. John was a craftsman, Joseph a labourer, and Joseph believed that John looked down on him. One night, driven to fury by John's condescension, Joseph took up his hammer and brought it down once, twice, three times on John's head until John stopped talking, and moving.'

Sarah glanced at the children, a boy and a girl. Was this really suitable? They seemed to be lapping it up, though.

'But what to do with the body?' the guide went on. 'There was one very simple solution. Joseph bricked John up in the walls of the half-built minster, where he lies to this day. Sometimes, on still nights, you can hear a voice on the wind. "*Help me*," it cries. "*Help me*." He held up a finger and they listened for a moment, but all Sarah could hear was Tom rustling in his pocket and then blowing his nose.

'Onwards!' cried the guide.

Away they trooped down one of the narrow streets leading away from the minster. Nothing looked familiar to Sarah, which maybe wasn't surprising, given that the only other time she and Tom had been to the city was more than thirty years ago. They'd stayed in a tiny B&B, their first weekend away. First time they'd slept in a double bed together. First time she'd slept in a double bed full stop. They'd barely left it that whole weekend. Though there was that strange moment when she'd stood at the window and seen a woman staring up at her. Thinking it must be someone she knew, Sarah raised her hand, but then the woman stepped back, into the road, and an oncoming car had only just stopped short of hitting her.

'Come closer,' the guide beckoned. 'Are we all here? One, two, three ... twelve, thirteen, plus me. Have we gained someone along the way? Never mind, at least we haven't lost anyone.'

Tom slipped on a cobblestone and Sarah shot out a hand to steady him. 'What would I do without you?' he said, gathering himself.

The street was so narrow, the buildings on either side almost met above their heads. A solitary lamppost illuminated the gloom. Sarah wrapped the darkness around her like a blanket.

'A tunnel runs under here,' Ishmael/Bob said. 'Some say it stretches from the minster to the river and was a route for smugglers. But it was closed up and for centuries nobody could locate it. On a night very like tonight, three lads newly turfed out from a tavern spotted a doorway, just here, that they'd never seen before. The door was unlocked, the hinges creaking, creaking as they pushed it open. Darkness, complete and utter.'

He paused. The kids were rapt. The hen party swayed, and the young couple kissed, half hidden by a raised umbrella.

'But one of the lads wasn't afraid,' the guide went on. 'He laid a bet that the doorway led to the old smugglers' tunnel. He'd go down and report back. He had with him a penny whistle and bade his friends follow his tune from above ground. He disappeared into the black, tootling his tune. His friends followed the sound, twenty yards, thirty, but the sound grew fainter, then stopped.'

'Did he die?' the small boy said.

'Who knows?' the guide replied. 'For he was never seen again. One of the friends fetched a lantern but when they returned to the doorway, they found no trace of a tunnel ever having been there.'

The boy shrank back into his mother's midriff.

'Let us continue,' Ishmael/Bob said. 'And as we do so, we should remember this: Wherever we go, whatever we do, we leave an impression, an imprint for later generations to see. Like footprints that never get washed away. Some say that this is what ghosts are — echoes of what came before ...'

* * *

'That's what we'd have ended up doing if we'd stuck to the acting,' Tom said later as they studied their menus in the Chinese by the castle. 'Cheesy ghost walks.'

'It's a living,' Sarah said. She meant it as a joke, but Tom didn't laugh.

After ordering, they sat in silence. Someone had told her once that this was the sign of a strong relationship: the ability to be comfortable in silence. But she was not comfortable, and it didn't look like Tom was either. He pulled off his jumper and draped it over the back of his chair. He rolled up his shirt sleeves as if he was about to punch someone. A sheen of perspiration formed on his forehead. She had loved the way his fringe fell almost into his eyes, but when he pushed it back now it stuck to his forehead.

They'd almost got through the main course when Tom said, 'Listen, I'm sorry. I really am. I don't know how many times I have to say it.'

'You don't have to keep saying it.'

'But I don't feel like you've forgiven me.'

'It's a lot to process,' she said.

'That's understandable.' He gulped at his wine, leaving a vampiric stain on his lips, then said, 'I thought maybe coming back here would be a good way of reconnecting us, you know? Reminding us of happier times.'

Happier times. She wondered if that was true. It *seemed* true. They had been hungry for each other. They'd had dreams, ambitions to make it big, turn their drama degrees into gold. But she remembered an overwhelming urge for the days to pass, to hurry up, to get to the future. She'd longed to be older.

He was on a roll now, asking if she remembered that time ... that time when ... when we did ... Do you remember? He scattered a whole host of memories around her, hoping that some of them would take root.

But there were alternative memories. She could have countered his with some of her own. Do you remember when you did that? Do you remember when you ...

Do you remember?

* * *

Back at the hotel, she filled the roll-top bath and slipped down into it. It was almost too hot to bear, but she made herself stay in. From the bedroom came bursts of tinny laughter, a choir singing, two men arguing, more laughter. Her body turned an angry shade of red. The scar on her abdomen remained white, though. She fingered the ridge of it, then ran her hands up and down her belly. She wondered how many layers of skin she had shed over the years. Her young skin gone, replaced by something drier, baggier. She kept renewing herself, but how long would she keep on doing that?

When she went into the bedroom, towel wrapped tightly around her, Tom was lying on his back, eyes closed, breathing softly. He was still fully dressed. She was glad she hadn't washed her hair as she didn't want to wake him by using the hairdryer. The towel dropped away and she stood naked in front of him. He didn't stir. She aimed the remote at the TV, turning it black. After putting on her pyjamas, she slipped carefully under the duvet. Tom shifted and she held her breath, but he settled again. She switched off the light and blinked into the darkness.

She woke briefly in the night and found the other side of the bed empty. Tom did that sometimes, got up and wandered around when he couldn't sleep. But where was there to wander in the hotel room? The bathroom light was off, so where was he? It didn't matter, she didn't really mind, and she was too drowsy to puzzle it out anyway. She soon fell asleep again.

* * *

Next morning at breakfast, Tom said, 'Thought I'd do one of the history tours today. Fancy it?'

What was it with him and tours all of a sudden?

'You go,' Sarah said. 'I'll look round the shops.'

The streets seemed even narrower in the daylight, perhaps because they were even more crowded. She stepped off pavements, bumped into people and got bumped into. Apologies were mumbled or shouted. Her breath clouded in front of her, mixing with everybody else's. All this breath, hanging over them like a miasma. At least it wasn't raining.

She was soon lost. She turned a corner and barely registered the sign as she passed. Doubling back, she took a second look: *Bed and Breakfast*. Something caught her eye in one of the windows above: a young woman wearing tartan pyjamas. Sarah couldn't see the woman clearly. Was she waving? Sarah pulled her hand out of her pocket and raised it in reply. It wasn't really a wave, more a mirroring gesture.

A car horn blared behind her and only then did she realise she'd stepped back into the middle of the road. Now she held up both her hands to the driver. For a moment, she thought he was going to shout at her, but he drove off. Sarah looked back up at the window, but the young woman was gone.

Sarah saw the minster over the roof of the B&B. She made her way towards it, keeping it in sight, until she found herself in familiar streets again. Soon she was back at the hotel. In the room, she stood at the window, but nobody waved at her. She packed quickly, not bothering to fold her clothes. Downstairs, she left her key with the receptionist, but didn't explain anything and the receptionist didn't ask.

Out in the city for the last time, she set off for the station. She thought of the builder buried behind the minster wall, the whistle player in the tunnel under her feet. Trapped.

Her phone buzzed but she ignored it. *Happier times*, she thought to herself. *Yes.*

Tina Morganella's story concludes our anthology by taking us back a couple of years, to a time of watching and waiting ...

The Loop
Tina Morganella

His tall, broad frame took up all the space in front of the fridge. When he sat on the sofa, his long legs sprawled under the coffee table and the toes of his battered sneakers poked out the other side. A black vinyl guitar case, covered in graffiti, was propped up alongside him. He looked down at his hands resting on his knees, and then glanced up at me. His mouth twisted an apology and he shrugged.

He was stuck in Australia, a friend of a friend. I had a spare room. How long could lockdown possibly last?

He wasn't chatty, wasn't happy with his thick accent. Sometimes he shut his eyes, searching his mind for the right word. I studied his face as I waited. After a moment, he would smile broadly, all teeth, and pronounce: Carpet. Pineapple. Tongs.

One night, after we'd exhausted all the free-to-air TV, and with no streaming channels to speak of, I introduced him to Window

Swap. I found this website where people from all over the world submit a clip of the view from their window. You press a button and a new vista appears.

We were both hooked.

During the day, I worked from home at the kitchen table. He watched TV or read my old paperbacks, to improve his English. Sometimes he wrote fractions of songs, plucking at the guitar strings. 'Is okay?' he would ask. I would nod, or else gently hold up a hand if I was on a Zoom meeting. He would go for long walks then, walks that weren't allowed.

But every night, after Uber Eats washed down with Coke, we settled in for a long session of Window Swap.

At first, we thought the views were streamed in real time and we watched eagerly, as though each scene was the opening credits of a movie. A busy street in Barcelona. A children's park in Seoul. We waited for the protagonist, the good guy or the bad guy, to show up with a gun, with a single rose, with a shout.

We were both disappointed when we recognised the same balding man with the green shirt walking down a street in Minsk over and over, and we realised each window was just a ten-minute recorded loop.

We put away ideas about potentially witnessing murders or catching out cheating couples. Instead, we watched cats on windowsills in Lisbon, or screaming kids in schoolyards in Copenhagen. It was almost always sunny in France and Morocco, but in Bangalore it rained a lot.

We set up the laptop and a bag of chips between us and took turns pressing the 'Open another window' button. Each download pause was filled with a snag of tension. Some window views were boring and static, others were lively. After a while the process became hypnotic. One more, just one more before bed.

Bucharest, Romania.

'Urgh!' He screwed up his face. 'There,' he pointed at the screen. 'Food poisoning. Hospital.' He shook his head at the memory, his curls bouncing around his temples.

Manchester, UK.

'I broke up with my boyfriend there,' I told him. One of the loneliest train rides of my life. I cried all the way from Manchester Piccadilly to Manchester Airport. He frowned at me in sympathy.

'I'm sorry,' he said. He touched my leg for a moment, then quickly pulled his hand away.

Morocco: he had his wallet stolen.

Hong Kong: I was offered a ride in a Ferrari but turned it down. He raised his eyebrows at me in surprise. Why? Because I didn't know the price I'd have to pay for the privilege. He snorted with laughter and nodded. 'Good.'

One twilight, I suggested we could submit the view from my second story flat. He strode over to the window, carefully held back the cream muslin curtain and pursed his lips. A paved courtyard with the neighbour's wattle tree hanging over the fence. Red bricks and three council-issued bins. But there were always rosellas with their beaks in the flowers, piping shrikes sometimes. He shrugged his shoulders and sat down again and opened another window.

But then he got up again, restless, arms folding and unfolding. As though, by looking out of our own, real window, he'd only just realised we were trapped for a good while longer. He paced around the tiny lounge room, his body expanding right up into the corners.

Then he threw himself down on the couch again, frowning. Rigid. 'I want to go.'

My heart seized. Of course. 'Soon, I'm sure.'

* * *

Shimmering lakes and hazy mountains. It seemed impossible that these homes could be anything but happy, optimistic. We couldn't imagine domestic violence or addiction going on behind the cameras, from this side of the windowsills.

Smoke from chimneys in the Czech Republic. A line of apartment buildings like broken teeth in Nairobi, Kenya. A tree-lined avenue in Aland Island, Finland. Places we had to Google. Sometimes we each listed all the countries we still needed to visit. But we didn't talk about how long it had been since we'd heard an A330 overhead, bound for Singapore, Qatar, Hong Kong.

Night after night, we often sat in silence now, opening one window after another, smiling at the screen, at each other. We played a game of snap, seeing who could shout 'I've been there!' first.

Sunny patios. A dog chasing a tennis ball into a pool over and over again.

He told me that growing up he had a cat with one eye called — he checked his translator — Blink. We burst out laughing. I teared up telling him about Trixie, our beautiful Kelpie. When I was twelve, we had to have her put down at the vet because she was riddled with cancer. I held Trixie in my arms as they gave her the injection. I don't know why they let me do that.

He reached over the middle cushion sofa that still divided us and squeezed my hand. He left it there, in mine.

In quiet countrysides the only sound was the wind on the microphone. In Mumbai, Moscow, Singapore, we heard the cars whooshing through rain sodden streets, horns tooting for friends or in anger. People shouted, laughed down below or across the way. We made up stories about the person behind the camera too. Did they set it up and walk away to have a shower, or did they sit and watch with us? Some of them played music. A woman (I'm sure it was a woman) played an old recording of 'La Vie en Rose' in Paris.

Then Yoshkar-Ola, Russia.

Bleak, grey sky, twilight. Drizzling. Dirty white tenement buildings, no one on the streets. I heard him gasp, 'Home.' It was his town. He stared hard, his face going from white to red. His mouth hung open a little, as though he wanted to say something. Tears collected in the corners of his eyes. On the couch, he slowly slid sideways and rested his head in my lap, one arm slid behind my back to hug me. I brushed the curls away from his ears, gently kissed his neck and stroked his forehead. We stayed like that until my thigh went numb. I needed to move, but when I glanced down, his eyes were still fixed on the screen.

There were no flights available yet. I held my breath.

One night a snowy Manhattan scene. After a few minutes, he went to change the window but I stayed his hand, asked him to wait. I was transfixed by the snow. We watched a woman wearing a full-body rabbit costume, complete with the head, walking down the street. The ubiquitous FedEx van pulled up, delivered a package and drove away. Cars crawled cautiously towards the intersection; a man walked his dog, who must have been cold without a jacket. Another man shovelled snow away from the entrance to a café. He scooped methodically, even though it was still snowing heavily. He would clear the way, and then the loop would start again so that it seemed he would never finish.

We watched the clip for over an hour.

About the Contributors

Eva Carson was born in Glasgow in 1984 and now lives in Fife. She's inspired by the spooky and the strange, towns and cities, and stories of the coast. Her stories have been published by *Carmen et Error* and *404 Ink Magazine*. She can be found online at evacarson.com.

Alastair Chisholm writes short stories and children's books. His picture book *Inch and Grub* won the Scottish Book Trust Bookbug Prize and the Queen's Knickers Award, and his children's science fiction novel *Orion Lost* was nominated for the Carnegie Medal.

Alastair lives in Edinburgh with his wife, family, and a cat, and he thinks it's weird to refer to himself in the third person. He likes biscuits.

About the Contributors

Ian Critchley is a freelance editor and journalist. His fiction has been published in several journals and anthologies, including *Neonlit: Time Out Book of New Writing, Volume 2*, *The Mechanics Institute Review #15*, *Structo*, *Lighthouse*, and *Litro*. He has won both the Hammond House International Literary Prize and the HISSAC Short Story Prize. His story 'Removals' is published as a limited-edition chapbook by Nightjar Press.

Jo Gatford writes flash disguised as poetry, poetry disguised as flash, and sometimes things that are even longer than a page. Her work has been published widely, and has most recently been selected for the wigleaf Top 50, Best Microfictions and Best Small Fictions 2024. Her hybrid chapbook, *The Woman's Part*, was published by Stanchion in 2023 and her novel, *White Lies*, was published by Legend Press in 2014.

In 2023 Jo won the Fiction Desk Writer's Award for her short story Yellow Rock, which appeared in *New Ghost Stories IV*. She writes about writing at 'The Joy of Fixion' on Substack, and edits other people's words for her supper at www.jogatford.com.

David Malvina writes short fiction and recently finished writing a novel. He moved to Yorkshire a few months ago after many years living in Hackney.

Tina Morganella is a freelance copy editor and writer. Her short fiction, personal essays and travel literature have appeared in *STORGY Magazine* (UK), *Entropy* (US), *Sudo* (Australia), *Litro* (UK/US), *Fly on the Wall Press* (UK), *Crannog* (Ireland) and the *2021 Newcastle Short Story Award Anthology* (Australia), amongst others, and her work was long listed for the Commonwealth Short Story Prize in 2022. Tina also has nonfiction work published in the Australian press (*The Big Issue*, *The Australian*, *The Adelaide Advertiser*).

Lauren O'Donoghue is a writer, game designer and community worker based in Yorkshire. Her previous and upcoming short fiction publications include *Horror Library Vol. 8*, *ergot.*, *Atlas & Alice*, *Blood Orange Review* and *Planet Scumm*. She is a candidate in the Curtis Brown Creative Breakthrough Programme, a writer for a US-based text game developer, and a freelance arts workshop facilitator.

For more information on the contributors to this volume, please visit our website:

www.thefictiondesk.com/authors

Also Available

the first fifteen Fiction Desk anthologies:

1. Various Authors
2. All These Little Worlds
3. The Maginot Line
4. Crying Just Like Anybody
5. Because of What Happened
6. New Ghost Stories
7. There Was Once a Place
8. New Ghost Stories II
9. Long Grey Beard and Glittering Eye
10. Separations
11. New Ghost Stories III
12. And Nothing Remains
13. Somewhere This Way
14. Houses Borders Ghosts
15. New Ghost Stories IV

www.thefictiondesk.com